THE HEROES

& Other Stories

Kat Hausler

ISBN 13: 978-0-9840984-4-6
ISBN: 0-9840984-4-5
Library of Congress Control Number: 2009907617

Cover design by All Things That Matter Press
Cover art by: Laurel Hausler http://laurelhausler.com/
Author photo by: Florian Boillot
Printed in 2009 by All Things That Matter Press

For my family,
and for my dear friends
in Virginia, New York, Berlin,
or anywhere else in the world they may wander to.

Acknowledgments

I'd like to thank all the wonderful teachers and mentors I've had over the years, especially Miranda McLeod, Elke Siegel, Ruth Danon, Rebekah Anderson, Amber West, Adam Wiedewitsch and Irini Spanidou. I'd also like to acknowledge the immeasurable kindness and encouragement I've received from my family and friends, and to assure them that if they recognize their own hairstyle or manner of speaking in a character of mine, anything further is fiction, and the allusion is meant with love. Last but certainly not least, I owe a thank you to 42 Magazine, where my fiction first appeared in print, and to my fellow writer Will Stamp for his ongoing help reviewing my work.

Table of Contents

Sheila stooped to pick up the two carry-on items permitted her. She pulled the strap of her laptop case—heavy with items that had nothing to do with computers, but hadn't fit into her other bag—over her shoulder, then strained to pick up the second, larger bag. Glanced at her desk to see whether she'd forgotten anything, or rather, whether she'd forgotten anything in sight, because, without having left her apartment, she was already sure of leaving something vital behind.

Her winter parka, lined in imitation fur, hung over the shoulders of her chair. If it'd had eyes, she thought, it might've thrown her an accusing look for trying to leave it behind. She sighed, removed herself from the two bags, put on the coat, and started again. She couldn't help but think of all the steps that lay between her and her destination: four flights of stairs; hailing a taxi—did they take credit cards?— the ride to JFK; finding the terminal; finding the gate, boarding the plane, but first waiting, waiting, waiting. A seven hour flight and then start all over again in Amsterdam. But she wouldn't think that far ahead yet. She looked forward to those seven hours in which she couldn't be expected to accomplish anything. In the close space of her bedroom, she sweated into her coat, but it would be cold in Russia.

As usual, Simon was still asleep on the living room sofa, though it was a Tuesday and already afternoon. Generally, Sheila tiptoed about the apartment, overcome with guilt at every creak of the floor, at every rattled dish, especially at the front door that screamed no matter how gently she eased it shut. But today she was deliberately noisy, stomping and rustling into the middle of the living room. She stood and waited for Simon to open his eyes and admit he was awake. It was their habitual practice for her to look away when she accidentally woke him, and for him to pretend he'd slept through the disturbance. But Sheila had told Simon the night before that she'd wake him up before leaving.

Earlier, while Simon still had the covers pulled over his head, Sheila had pictured a charming scene in which she gave him a quick kiss — perhaps on the mouth, but more likely on the cheek — on her way out. It had seemed appropriate, the right start to her journey.

Now, as Simon opened his pink-tinted eyes and stared up at her from the sofa, she saw how ridiculous the thought had been. She must not allow herself to mistake their domesticity, their friendly familiarity, for intimacy. The recollection of her fantasy embarrassed her; she and Simon would not be able to live together if she developed those kinds of feelings for him. Setting aside the impossibility of his reciprocating a romantic interest, she wasn't even attracted to him. Simon was too blonde, too deliberately scraggly, wore his clothes too tight, and was altogether too effete for Sheila's taste. It was only that she'd been lonely, had pictured to herself the scene of the lovers' goodbye, and had no one to cast in the male part except Simon.

She imagined Simon sometimes felt the same way about her, in a way that transcended matters of gender. He'd once remarked that an old army shirt she'd bought at a thrift shop reminded him of his ex-boyfriend. Sheila had felt uncomfortable and not worn the shirt since. Other times, when they talked or watched TV together at night, Simon sat very close to her, his arm not yet around her, but almost, poised over the back of the sofa as if en route, her shoulder the final destination it never quite made. Sheila didn't mind because she knew he didn't mean anything by it. She knew he was thinking about Gregory and she didn't want him to feel lonely.

The kind of lonely someone like Simon might feel was different from the kind of lonely Sheila had grown used to, because Simon really knew what he was missing. Gregory and Simon had lived together for two years before Gregory split for Los Angeles and left Simon looking for somebody's sofa to crash on. Simon never used the word love when he talked about Gregory, but Sheila could tell he meant it. It had been hard to find ways to cheer him up afterwards, and he'd always been such a happy person. People who were capable of that kind of emotional attachment were also, in Sheila's opinion, capable of more intense suffering. In the short run, anyway.

"I'm going to Russia, Simon," she said, because she knew he'd forgotten.

"Wow." He closed his eyes as he thought about this, and she wondered whether he would fall asleep again. "Well, have a safe trip."

"Thanks." When he didn't say anything else, Sheila tensed her muscles under the weight of her bags and walked out of the apartment. So much for goodbyes.

"I'll see you," she called over the scream of the closing door. She didn't hear an answer.

***

In the taxi on the way to JFK the driver asked Sheila where she was from, and she considered that this was the first real conversation she'd had with anyone all day, though she'd been up since nine. Ordering a cup of coffee and advising Simon of her departure didn't count.

"I live in the East Village," was her first line of defense. She didn't wish to be mistaken for a tourist. After three years in the city, Sheila felt she'd done her time. "But I'm from DC originally," she added, wanting to be polite. The answer was a compromise; she was actually from an upper-middle class Virginia suburb, but she thought saying 'DC' made her sound tougher, street-savvier, less like a dreamy-eyed Southerner still wet behind the ears with sweet tea. She wasn't as offended by the man's question as she would have been, had he not clearly been born outside of Manhattan.

"Virginia?" he asked.

Sheila thought this at first uncanny, then recalled that he'd had a fifty-fifty chance of guessing right.

"PG County," she named a district of Maryland, which, in her low-minority, high-income county, was considered dangerous. Immediately she regretted the lie. Why had she cared enough what this incidental stranger thought to lie to him?

"Virginia?" the driver repeated as they cruised uptown, and she saw that this was neither an accusation of dishonesty, nor an invitation to redeem herself. He simply didn't know which state the county was in. His heavy accent softened the name: 'Wejinya'. She guessed he was maybe from India, but what did she know about that part of the world?

"Yeah, Northern Virginia," she agreed, relieved at the chance to take back the lie without being caught in it. The driver disjointedly detailed his experiences in a nearby county. Sheila pretended to be interested, tried to think of things to say.

"That's a nice area," she said, though she found it as dry and lifeless as her own hometown. She thought the subject exhausted, and wondered what else they could discuss. It seemed it was her turn to introduce something.

"Where are you from?" She felt all right asking because he'd asked first. Otherwise she would've worried about sounding racist, patronizing. Sheila thought of her mother, who asked every person with an accent what country he or she came from, as if she were collecting quaint exoticisms.

"Bangladesh," the driver replied, and then went on to describe it. Sheila could think of nothing to say but, 'Oh,' and this seemed insufficient. The driver had lived in Brooklyn for almost twenty years. He, too, was defensive about his right to call New York home.

Sheila was out of topics, so she looked out the window at the store fronts and pedestrians they passed heading across town. Hoped they'd sink into a comfortable silence.

"Are you student?" the driver asked.

Sheila felt tempted to lie again. She hated introducing herself as a student; it seemed to take away from her credentials not just as a New Yorker, but also as an adult. She didn't like to be relegated to a caste that implied she was still developing, wasn't a fully-formed person yet. It was unfair that high school dropouts with minimum wage jobs and no prospects could consider themselves more adult than she. But her prejudice towards higher education reeked of bourgeois snobbery, and she swept the thought into an obscure corner.

"And I work in marketing," she added, to assuage her damaged self-worth. There was a kernel of truth under the pulpy flesh of fabrication; she did hand out promotional flyers for hourly pay. This lie, though, confused Sheila more than the last. She considered people who lied to make their jobs sound more impressive pathetic.

"Where you are going?" The driver wasn't interested in her professional pretensions.

"Russia." She hoped he wouldn't bore her with questions about her travel plans. The trip was so short that any great discussion of it seemed out of proportion. She wondered why it exhausted her so much to make small talk, and resolved to work harder.

"Wacation?"

"I have an internship," she replied, deliberately self-important. Here was a question she was happy to answer. Along with spending money and straight A's, the week-long academic internship to which Sheila had been accepted in Moscow was one of few things she felt she'd ever earned for herself. And she had earned it, had deserved it.

It was a joke Sheila made too often that she put all her romantic energy into her studies. Certainly, she wasn't putting it anywhere else. But she had high hopes for this trip. If only for a week, she could pretend to be someone alluring, even lovable. Her fellow students—from all over the world—would surely not have the narrow interests of the young men she knew in America, whose unidentifiable focus somehow cut her out of every scene. Sheila wanted friends who would remember her fondly after the end of the practicum, but more than that she hoped to make that special kind of connection, the one she couldn't quite latch onto here. She'd had little to no luck with dating, but felt sure that, in a new context, with all the potential packed into a mere seven days, she could wring a few drops of passion from her life.

Sheila often remarked that she hated being single, and was surprised and a little offended that none of her friends ever set her up on a date. They all seemed to take her loneliness for granted, to see it as an inherent part of her.

When the driver didn't respond, she wondered whether he were genuinely interested in her life, or only felt obligated to make conversation with his passengers. If Sheila were a taxi driver, she'd collect stories from the more interesting people she picked up. Reflecting on the information she'd provided, she regretted that she wouldn't be included in such a collection.

Sheila's thoughts came to a focus again when the driver resumed speaking. She was about to ask him what he'd said, but then realized he was speaking—in whatever language they speak in Bangladesh; she had no idea—into a hands-free telephone. The realization came to her clearly as a written word: She hadn't been interesting enough for him. The bare edge of regret pressed into her unspeaking throat, and she struggled to breathe silently, to persuade herself that she was only nervous about her flight.

The driver continued to hold intermittent cell phone conversations the rest of the way to the airport. Occasionally, he glanced at Sheila in the rearview mirror, in which she could see her own wispy brown hair, the white scalp of her part. From his angle the driver could probably see all of her. She wondered whether he found her attractive. Hers was an idle, intellectual curiosity; it didn't occur to her to consider him as a potential object of her own interest. He was too old, too far outside the realm of Sheila's acquaintances. And Sheila wasn't accustomed to a mutual sense of attraction.

***

Seated by the window on the airplane, Sheila experienced the relief she'd looked forward to. She hadn't yet recalled anything important left behind, and could now relax for a few hours. Pretending to read, she watched the seats next to her, hoping for a handsome young neighbor. An older businessman sat in the aisle seat. The one between them remained empty and Sheila felt more disappointed than she'd expected to. She stopped pretending and read in earnest, making the triumphs and pitfalls of the characters her own.

She became very thirsty but didn't want to bother anyone. When the bustling Dutch stewardess came around with the drink cart, Sheila asked so quietly for a glass of water that the woman couldn't tell which language she was speaking.

The cart came around again later with liquor, and the businessman ordered a brandy. The stewardess didn't offer Sheila anything, and she felt slighted. While she didn't want to drink alone on the plane, she was twenty-two and wanted to be taken for the adult that she was. She considered ordering a drink out of spite, just to get out her ID and show it to the woman, but what would that have accomplished? She'd only have ended up drinking alone on an airplane, feeling sorry for herself.

She settled into her seat, wondered if she should make conversation with the businessman after a while. Cell phones weren't allowed, so she thought she might ask him what time it was. She hadn't wanted a chatty seatmate, but she was tired of the emotional engagement of reading, tired of conjuring up characters she'd never meet. Besides, there was only one story left, and she wanted to save it for later. It wouldn't make sense to have brought the book at all, if she finished it before she arrived.

Sheila looked out the window, but it was cloudy and almost dark. The screens over the aisles were playing a romantic comedy she had no interest in watching. A few times she looked up to see whether she could guess what the Dutch subtitles meant. Here and there the meaning of one or two words leapt out at her, but never whole sentences.

Sheila paged through the in-flight magazine, whose theme this month was happiness. It featured pictures of happy couples from around the world, and a few very unscientific articles on the origin of the emotion. Sheila read one entitled 'What Makes Us Happy?' She'd been wondering that herself.

The article was largely based on opinion polls and made unrelated remarks, such as that people were less happy in hot climates and more happy if they were tall. A sidebar commented that extroverted people were happier than introverts because their better social skills offered them a wider range of experiences.

Sheila was intellectually offended. A correlation might be shown to exist between level of extroversion and *reported* level of happiness, but the conclusion that followed could never be empirically proven. Perhaps extroverted people only reported themselves happier, because they never took the time to think about it. Sheila next asked herself why she was bothering to argue with this fluffy publication whose main function was providing a catalogue of duty-free items for sale on the plane. She put the magazine back into the seat-pocket in front of her.

The stewardess returned with Sheila's special vegetarian meal. With difficulty Sheila balanced the crowded tray while she opened the folding table in front of her. She could've set the tray on the table of the middle seat, but the businessman had taken that over with his belongings, and she didn't want to inconvenience him. He didn't have a meal yet, and neither did any other passenger Sheila could see.

She hesitated. It was difficult to overcome the sense that it would be rude to eat before the others were served. Once she'd begun eating, she made a slow pantomime of picking at her food, forcing herself to display minimal interest in spite of having skipped lunch. She worried that people in front of whom she ate found her unappealing, and didn't want to seem too eager, like a dog gobbling up whatever was put in front of it. Somewhere she'd gotten the idea that ladies had birdlike appetites. When she caught herself bending over the tray, she felt disgusted. Leaning back in her seat, she picked at her fruit salad until the businessman received his dinner, then discreetly ate a buttered role.

Sheila thought this might be easier if she were a male. Rarely had she noticed a man or boy shy about eating in public. She remembered a thin, ill-kempt young man, George, whom she'd met on a flight back from Italy her freshman year of college. He'd told her hours of stories about his travels. He'd been all over, and even taught English in Vietnam and Cambodia. She'd found him somewhat self-involved, but interesting.

When the meal trays arrived, George had indiscriminately finished off everything on his, and then what Sheila hadn't eaten from hers. He explained that sometimes the airline would give you an extra meal if you asked. Sheila had been appalled at the thought of asking for more food, the appearance of greed or the need to beg for charity. But then she'd respected George, one of few people she'd met who knew the worth of a meal, had probably skipped enough to learn it.

The businessman next to Sheila didn't seem self-conscious either, little as he looked as if he'd ever gone hungry. Nor did he have any visible qualms about traveling alone. The thought that this would be easier if she were a man reminded Sheila of another recurrent thought: that this would be easier if she were *with* a man. Not because he'd do anything Sheila couldn't do herself, but because, with him in tow, Sheila would be able to do anything she wanted, confident of the only kind of approval she truly craved, and for which everything else seemed a cheap and flimsy consolation prize.

Sheila fell asleep after they'd taken away her tray, and never succeeded in asking the businessman for the time. On her connecting flight to Moscow, she again waited for a handsome and companionable seatmate, was again disappointed. She satisfied herself with the hope of some racy fling abroad, and slept again. Her dreams didn't relate to her earlier thoughts, and on waking she berated her subconscious for its deeply ingrained perception of her as single. Not even in her imagination could she be with someone. Sheila passed through customs half-asleep, aware only of the shuffling line, the firm click of the stamp being pressed against her passport.

In the terminal, she looked around for her group, and was disappointed to notice that Sheremetyvo International looked almost exactly like every other airport she'd been in. The only difference was that the letters in the shop windows looked upside down or backwards. But the hurrying, happy, or anxious people were the same as in New York, as anywhere. It didn't matter what language the clouds of conversation blew by in; no one was speaking to her.

Sheila made her way to the baggage claim. She'd packed everything in her two carry-ons, but thought the dozen or so others might have luggage. Sure enough, the familiar English letters of a hand-written sign soon called her to the baggage conveyor. Next to the sign, a gaunt, dark-haired man leaned against a large red suitcase, waiting either for a second bag or the rest of the group. He looked intelligent, but not very old. Sheila couldn't tell whether he was one of the group leaders, or a student. She hoped he was a student. Already as she approached she found him striking, and now that they were closer, within range of real contact, she was sure that their arrival ahead of the others must be some sign, that certain indefinable something she'd come all this way looking for.

His eyes were dark and flowing, a waterfall of a gaze that caught her own, then spilled down to the dusty plastic floor. Sheila was sure she recognized something in that look, a kind of reflection and an unexpected presence, clear as a spoken greeting. She was startled, as if, strolling down a desolate side street, she'd suddenly collided with someone she knew.

She watched him a moment, waiting for him to speak. Then he turned to stare at the slow, creaking motion of the conveyor belt, and she realized he wasn't going to.

"Hi," she managed, and for this effort was rewarded with a vague grunt. She asked whether he were with the program, received a nod. What was she doing wrong? Sheila put down her bags. She didn't want him to catch her looking at him, now that she had no more questions ready, so she followed his example, and stared at the conveyor. The circling luggage was rather picked over now; most people had claimed what was theirs and left. The remnants were by and large black rolling suitcases, streaked with dust and scuffed on their plastic wheels. Sheila noticed a tan leather case, almost too small to have been checked at all, on its side apart from the others. It made the circuit as she watched, and continued unretrieved, even as the belt began to display the next set of luggage.

Sheila felt antsy, as if she'd forgotten something important. The tan case passed again, now crowded in on both sides by larger baggage. It occurred to Sheila that she'd neglected to introduce herself, hadn't even asked for his name. How were they supposed to have any kind of connection without knowing one another's names? How was she supposed to get to know anyone if she couldn't manage such a simple, obvious step? Sheila tried to collect herself and deliver the needed words, but couldn't decide whether it weren't already too late. How long had they stood here, silent? Wasn't there already some insurmountable barrier between them? She felt as if she'd disappointed the young man from the beginning. The tan case passed again, and Sheila feigned a cough, in case he'd look up.

When he did, she swallowed dry, and tried to begin something. "I'm Sheila. What's your name?"

She couldn't tell whether it was her nervousness or some particular complexity of his answer that kept her from understanding.

"What?"

"Alyosha," he repeated.

"Oh." Sheila thought he sounded annoyed, and wished she'd waited, had pretended to understand and then later read his name off some list. Surely they'd call attendance. She'd botched the situation terribly. Why should he bother speaking if she weren't listening? But she was, she was listening, even listening too carefully. At the same time, she wasn't at all sure he'd understood her name. She'd spoken so softly, let the syllables run into each other. Alyosha couldn't have understood. That he didn't ask again meant he didn't care. She'd try again; she had to. Surely there was something. Where were all the others? That was valid, a perfectly acceptable thing to say. And she almost said it.

But Alyosha didn't appear to share either her curiosity, or her interest in forming a closer acquaintance. With a stiff 'Excuse me,' he took his dark flowing eyes and his large red suitcase and walked off. Sheila tried to explain this to herself. Maybe he had to use the bathroom, or wanted to buy something from a convenience store. It couldn't be she was really that intolerable. Could it? They should've spoken more. No, it was her fault. She'd started the conversation and should've said more, come up with something interesting. But he'd seemed to have so little to say to her.

Maybe he didn't speak very much English, and had been embarrassed. That could be. The program was conducted in English, but Alyosha might not have felt up to conversing with a native speaker right away. She should've spoken more clearly, so as not to intimidate him. That had to be it, a matter of language. How silly, though. Sheila wouldn't have minded if he made a mistake here or there; she only wanted to keep and be kept company. And now he'd gone off, even if only for a few minutes, and the conversation was closed. Sheila wished she knew Russian, so she could've surprised and impressed him, spoken to him in his own language. Learning French had never seemed such a waste of time. Surely, though, they could've understood enough, didn't need fluency on either side to get acquainted. Weren't there other ways to communicate—with the eyes, a smile, simple physical proximity? Sheila recalled the sense of his look cascading over hers, and contented herself with the thought that they'd said as much to each other as it was possible for them to say.

Young men and women began to trickle over, asking each other hushed questions, struggling with baggage. Sheila glanced around, waiting for Alyosha's return. She'd do better when he got back, try harder. They'd be friends because they'd met first, and back in America she'd remember his gaunt, handsome face, the graceful way he spoke his name. As to the new arrivals, Sheila didn't attempt to strike up any conversations. Having already exerted her capacities to the fullest, she waited for someone to speak to her. But no one even looked. Sheila didn't know which way to face without seeming to stare, so she turned back to the conveyor, now plucked more bare than ever. Someone had retrieved the tan leather case, and she watched without anticipation the empty spot from which it had been pulled.

When Alyosha came back with a coffee and a Cyrillic newspaper, she tried to meet his eyes and smile, let him know he didn't have to be perfect for her, grammatically or otherwise. But he didn't look in her direction, instead struck up a conversation with the students nearest him. He spoke an agile, practiced English, and even broke into laughter several times, his expression warm as Sheila hadn't imagined it before. Seeing that the errors of speech had all been hers, she resolved not to repeat them. Sheila fell into a deep and lasting silence, which, if anyone minded, at least no one attempted to lift her from.

An hour later, they arrived in Moscow proper, where neither a tempestuous affair, nor the briefest flirtation awaited Sheila. Russia was indeed very cold. In spite of hours of lectures and guided tours, she came home again feeling she'd learned nothing of value.

***

Simon was asleep again when Sheila and her suitcases clambered back up the stairs, but awoke at the scream of the door.

"Sorry," Sheila said, seeing his pink-rimmed eyes, their startled expression.

"You're back early."

"No," she told him. "This was always when I was coming back."

Simon checked the time, groaned, and settled back into his blankets. Sheila decided he probably still dreamt of Gregory, in the same way she sometimes woke confused at not finding herself in bed in Virginia. When Simon fell asleep again, Sheila took a shower and dressed. She put on her old army shirt. It couldn't do any harm.

Later Sheila and Simon sat together on the sofa watching a late night movie. He leaned against her shoulder, closed his eyes. Sheila thought how he was always tired, must stay up nights while she slept, to be so tired. His weight pulled at the sleeve of the faded green military shirt. When Simon closed his eyes, did her shoulder feel the same as Gregory's? Her arms were smaller in the loose cloth. But Simon was already asleep, and his dreams would fill in the empty fabric. Sheila switched off the TV. She wanted to fall asleep too, but she'd changed time zones too many times to have the option. She considered getting up, but every other place in the apartment seemed quiet, empty, cold. She leaned back against Simon and closed her eyes. Remembered the businessman who thought nothing of traveling alone. Maybe he'd been everywhere already. She wondered whether he ever had trouble falling asleep, or whether jetlag were something you developed immunity to.

Sheila thought of taking another trip; this one had been a blur of isolation, Moscow too familiar in its strangeness. She wanted to go somewhere no one spoke English, where no one had ever heard of Manhattan, so she'd have an excuse to be really alone. She wanted to find a place where the Alyoshas expressed whole conversations at a glance, and had names so foreign they'd never expect her to get them on the first try. A place where she'd recognize someone by a look, a touch, and find she wasn't alone after all, however far she'd traveled. To find a connection she could just feel, without needing to find the words for.

Sheila thought of all the exotic places she could get off a plane in. Her mind wandered to Bangladesh. She tried to place it on a map but couldn't. She thought George could've. Maybe he was there now, teaching English to future cabbies of New York. Did Wejinya sound as exotic to that taxi driver as Bangladesh did to her? Perhaps he'd made it his own, the outer limits of his new sense of home. Finally Sheila fell asleep against Simon.

She woke the next day late for her, early for him, and found that he'd wrapped an arm around her in his sleep, no doubt dreaming of happier times. She considered trying to wriggle out without waking him, but knew she wouldn't be able to, that he'd wake with first disappointment and then an apology. Better to let them both pretend a little longer. She closed her eyes again, imagined she and Simon were different people. And for a time they were. He was content to hold her, and she to be held.

In Color

Alex left the darkroom hopeful but uncertain. Reaching St. Mark's Place, he walked a little faster, stepping around aggressive street vendors in his eagerness to get home and evaluate the past week. He took the steps up to his apartment two and three at a time. Once inside, he sank down onto the off-white flannel sofa that he called the 'living room,' placed as it was in the center of a stained steel kitchenette. He pulled the folder out of his messenger bag. From their bedroom, he could hear his roommate Josh idly picking at a guitar.

Out of the photo folder came a sober-faced doorman in a long, button-up jacket and policeman's cap, guarding the dignity of his Fifth Avenue position; two children aiming toy guns between the Hudson and the West Side Highway, uninhibitedly bloodthirsty in their play; a Lower East Side prostitute of indeterminate age, her face hidden as she stooped to tie the broken lace on her short leather boot. The black-and-white prints effused vibrant life and the smell of chemical solutions. Alex shuffled further into his collection. A disreputable-looking man leaned over a park bench where a well-kempt girl read a Victorian novel, attempting to ignore his attentions. Nearby, a squirrel held a brazen staring contest with a lean old three-legged Dalmatian through the metal fence of the dog park. Alex took off his glasses and polished them on the hem of his blue windbreaker before paging onward.

Josh hopped clumsily out of the bedroom, kicking off a scuffed pair of jeans.

"Hey, man, new pictures? Pretty sweet." He made for the bathroom to brush his teeth and get in the shower.

"You're in this bunch, remember?" Alex knew Josh would take far greater interest in his work if it were centered on his favorite subject. Josh turned back and leaned against the sofa to look on with Alex.

"Man, that hurt," Josh recalled, looking at the next picture in the collection. Alex didn't usually take pictures of his friends unless he caught them by surprise, but he'd found the scene irresistibly aesthetic: Josh, pants down, tears in his eyes, washcloth in his teeth, holding tightly to two friends' hands, getting his first tattoo. The backdrop was the 'living room' of their apartment. It had been a very hands-on operation for the group in attendance; Josh's brother had personally applied the ink via a sewing needle, sterilized with a match and tied to the end of a broken pencil. Alex felt that this scene was certainly worth a thousand words, but was disappointed in its choice of vocabulary. Art photography wasn't about shock value, and he considered graphicness a cheap thrill for the viewer at the expense of something more transcendent.

After Josh's tattoo, came a couple running to catch a subway train already in motion. In her hurry the woman had grabbed the man's sleeve instead of his hand, and his coat was falling off towards her. They hadn't yet had time to realize they weren't going to make it. Motion-blurred faces from inside the train watched their impending disappointment, indifferent. In the next photo several barely-standing girls held back their friend's hair while she vomited into a gutter. The girls, even the one purging herself of what looked like a gallon of drinks, were beautiful and dressed at conspicuous expense. An immigrant mother and her young daughter looked back over their shoulders as they crossed the street away from the spectacle, staring without shame.

"These are really cool, Alex."

Alex blinked and looked up, having forgotten Josh's presence.

"No, they suck. I'm just seeing what everyone else sees."

"Picasso probably said some shit like that too, dude," were Josh's parting words. Alex waited until he heard the sound of the shower running, then hurried into the bedroom, where he deposited the folder with a pile of its kind in the bottom drawer of his desk.

"I hate Picasso," he said under his breath as he assembled his camera. In spite of Josh's occasionally warm support, Alex didn't find it worth his time to look through the rest of the pictures he'd developed early that afternoon—he knew he hadn't found what he was looking for. The brief note he left read:

'Went out. Later. -Alex.'

Without a destination in mind, Alex took off to find art, wherever it might be hiding. He didn't get far.

"Alex! Where have you been all weekend?!" an excited girl demanded, stopping him almost as soon as he'd stepped out of his apartment. Confused, he cleaned his glasses and put them back on, staring at her all the while. Naturally he recognized her; he just didn't know what she wanted. She stared back at him apoplectically.

"Well?"

"Around... is something the matter?" Alex wanted to look at his watch and see how much time he was wasting by taking part in this exchange, but he knew that would just make Sally angrier, which was the last thing he wanted to do. He frowned apologetically and tried to recall any possible cause of her displeasure, but was distracted by the passage of a B-list actress, and the wake of turning heads that followed her. A look of bitter envy passed over the face of a plain woman walking in the opposite direction; she leaned into her companion to make a snide remark. Alex shook his head, thinking what a picture it would've made.

"I just thought you were going to call me. You said you were going to call me," Sally was saying. Her straight blonde hair was blowing in the wind and she looked like she might cry out of spite. Alex ran his hands thoughtfully over his camera bag, but was dumbfounded by her accusation.

"I was going to call you?" He wished he could just refer her to Josh, who had far more experience in the field of theatrics. This kind of overacted scene was exactly what he wasn't looking for. As a photographer, Alex naturally preferred the stillness and essentialism of a distant image to this sentimental noise and motion now thrust in his face.

Sally breathed in sharply as if to dilute the concentration of her indignation. She spoke in small spurts of words.

"The other day, I said, we should, hang out, this weekend. You said, 'that sounds okay,' and I said, 'so call me,' and you said, you would, but you didn't."

Alex was dismayed at her hurt feelings and his lost time.

"I'm sorry; I guess I got busy. Next time that happens you should just call me." He was relieved to see two figures approaching, one of whom was his good friend Leila. The other was unfamiliar and largely concealed by an oversized snow hat, just too warm for the weather, and a padded parka which came down below her thighs.

"Leila! Hey!" Alex shouted enthusiastically, feeling himself on the point of extrication from an otherwise inescapable situation.

"Hey dude, what's up? This is Kelly." Leila, bundled into a colorfully vintage 1980's knit sweater, indicated the drooping ski hat, which nodded vaguely at the introduction.

"I'm Alex. This is Sally." The trick, Alex decided, was to get away from Sally before the other two left, assuming she had enough tact not to start a fight in front of a stranger. She knew Leila only in passing, and Kelly not at all. He looked at the new arrivals hopefully. Kelly had wide eyes and a narrow gap between her front teeth that she slid her tongue under when she smiled, a nervous gesture she repeated every few seconds.

"It's nice to meet you, Kelly. Do you mind if I take your picture?"

Kelly stammered something by way of permission, and Leila laughed jovially. "But not now, later," Alex added as everyone seemed to wait on him. Leila laughed again.

"You're weird, Alex. Is Josh home?"

Alex saw his window of opportunity to depart alone closing, and acted decisively. "Yeah, but he might still be in the shower. I've got to run. Nice seeing you ladies." Alex took off down the street as if he had a pressing appointment at the end of the block, but as soon as he turned onto Second Avenue and out of sight of the girls, he slackened his pace and began looking around for inspiration. Heading downtown, he captured a beat old deli of the archetypal New York mode, complete with two underage kids smuggling bottles of beer around the side of it; and an old Russian woman who stopped trying to sell handmade jewelry off a card table on the sidewalk to blow her nose into an embroidered black handkerchief.

Alex took a few moments between shots to cursorily approach the question of Sally. He didn't have room in his life for the kind of games she seemed to delight in playing, the ones she designed deep within some invisible lack of self worth. When they'd made that gradual transition from friends-of-friends to just friends, Alex had admired a certain brutal honesty in her attitude, but on the basis of her recent behavior he had to conclude that he'd been had. Sally merely said what she pretended to be thinking with enough conviction to pass it off. On top of which, she was becoming so needy that Alex could no longer avoid the pressing dread of her falling in love with him. It was a shame she'd become so difficult, since she was such a classically photogenic blonde. Still, her incongruous aptness as subject matter only further convinced Alex that he was better off sticking to his vision and those who could comprehend it.

Heading into the Lower East Side just as the sun was beginning to turn in for the evening, Alex stopped at the corner of a busy intersection. Curled up on the ground, a wiry old homeless man was smoking an absurdly long and thin cigarette, apparently of his own construction, and forming a decidedly semicircular shape from one end to the next. The old man was talking to himself excitedly beneath a broad and ancient fedora, but he broke off at Alex's approach.

"Wow, that's crazy." Alex admired the cigarette and the narrow stream of smoke funneling out from under the hat. "Could I get a picture?"

Alex got out his camera and snapped a few pictures as the man resumed his one-person dialogue. He was interrupted from further work when the bony fingers of his subject attempted to thrust their prize into his face.

"Have a smoke?" the bum offered courteously, having gained his footing.

"No, thank you," Alex replied, dodging his head to one side and taking another picture.

"Have a smoke," the bum repeated with no suggestion of a question. Alex laughed and shook his head. He spotted Leila and Kelly leaving the tea house down the street and waved, pleased with the coincidental encounter. Leila was the kind who understood things and never tried to get too close; he was always uncomplicatedly happy to see her. Kelly he couldn't come to a decision about just yet. He walked to the street corner to wait for them. The lean old man followed him, smoldering out of his fedora and—cigarette clutched in his teeth—disjointedly cursed today's youth, the government, freemasons and sundry mumbled institutions. The light changed, but the girls seemed in no hurry to reach him. Traffic was already flowing down Houston again by the time they made it to Alex's corner. He snapped a few pictures of the seedy booker across the street while he waited.

"Fancy meeting you here," Leila greeted him.

"Hey again." Kelly flicked her tongue under the gap in her teeth and looked nervously at the bum, who was leering into their group. Alex made a split-second decision to find her worthy of his companionship, if only as an accessory to Leila.

"Look at this guy, he's crazy," Alex boasted to the two girls, who laughed cautiously. The poor old guy had a piss stain on the front of his sagging pants. Alex had to get a full-body picture.

"Hey, you two just stand here for a second and keep him busy," he ordered Leila and Kelly. Eagerly he watched the old man spin into a tirade on women, all-but inaudible and unintelligible to anyone but himself.

"Umm…" Kelly mumbled in displeasure.

Alex stepped back to catch a picture of their discomfort as the old man gesticulated and waved his cigarette in their faces. He wondered what loud Leila was doing with such a timid friend, but then saw that even Leila had dropped her jaw. Still frantically snapping pictures, Alex located the source of their horrified expressions: The old man had unzipped the fly of his pants and his behavior had taken on a distinctly vulgar character.

"We're leaving, Alex!" Leila shouted, shaking her short black haircut at him as she turned away. She and Kelly linked arms and stepped into the street, dodging speeding cars in their eagerness to get away from the dirty old man, who showed every intention of following them.

Alex dashed after them and then ran ahead. He was torn between his awareness that the girls were frightened and angry, and his desire to get a picture of the bum exposing himself and then stalking them like a zombie into traffic, that funny cigarette still in his brown teeth.

"Come on, go with us," he called to the old man, pressing the shutter as fast as he was able, and knowing Leila wouldn't forgive him.

"*Alex!*" she hissed angrily.

"Oh, my." Kelly appeared to choose between collision with a speeding car and the man approaching two lanes away.

Alex took a step backwards to capture her wide look of revulsion just as the bum took a step towards them. Horns honked and brakes screeched. Alex and the bum flew in opposite directions as the girls stood on their island of safety, the thin line between the lanes. The drivers of a truck and a taxi respectively rushed out of their vehicles and onto the street, shouting. Kelly screamed. A flood of people left the surrounding sidewalks to gape at the scene. The two drivers both ran to Alex, neglecting the bum, whom only a passing policeman found worthy of notice, and then only long enough to observe that he was dead.

Alex, lying on his face, was the center of attention, the focal point of this picture, but not of the one he saw. Away from the broken lenses of his camera and glasses, he had finally found the perfect lighting, the perfect scene, and the perfect angle, all at once. He had never imagined that heaven came in black and white, yet he realized that he could never have doubted it. He looked down on the city from its greatest heights and he looked up from its depths, and all he saw was beauty. The people on the streets glowed as if their faces and bodies were only lanterns for some incomprehensibly bright flame within them. The sounds had ceased but there was one voice Alex could hear, a voice without words that became a face before his amazed eyes, assuring him of the perfection of all around him, and the love of the one who had put them there. Alex watched the face out of the corners of his eyes, as he could neither look away nor take in all of it at once.

The voice promised him something he hadn't known how to ask for, and the world around him began to change. Color leaked into the frame, brighter and more fiercely alive than seemed possible. Alex parted the dull body he'd inhabited this long as if it were so many cobwebs, and rose into the world of color and light. He felt himself burn with the glow he could see in those around him. Then the voice stopped speaking and the face melted into the palette around him. Alex began to hear earthly sounds again and the colors faded slowly to their ordinary hues.

"Please just one picture!" he cried out to the voice as all the images before him disappeared into black pavement. He felt his mortality flow back into him like the painful recirculation of blood into a limb that had fallen asleep.

"We know him, just tell us if he's okay," Alex heard Leila shouting at someone over the approaching scream of an ambulance. Firm gloved hands gripped and lifted him, restoring his view of his surroundings; they turned him over and placed him on a stretcher.

"I'm okay." He tasted the thickness of blood on his chipped teeth and felt it swamp his face. He tried to breathe through his nose and could not. He tried to see again the picture that had been shown to him, and could not. Leila and Kelly broke through the lines of EMT workers to reach his side.

"You're alright, dude, just hang in there," Leila told him.

Alex looked around at the faces hovering above him, seeing and not seeing that one perfect face in each of them. Newly aware that he hadn't died, he tried to place what kind of time this was, whether he should hold onto ecstasy or allow himself to despair.

"Picture. God." Alex tried to tell them about the glory he had seen, how close he'd been, but they misunderstood.

"Don't worry about that, Alex; you're lucky to be alive," were Leila's words of wisdom as Kelly, eyes narrowed and damp, held up his shattered camera.

Alex tried to reach for her hand, shaking, and knock the camera aside, but he could only raise a couple of fingers.

"You're gonna be fine." Leila nodded at him encouragingly.

Just before the two girls were shunted aside by his industrious rescuers, Alex, lisping through broken teeth and swollen lips, called Kelly over to tell her his secret. She blinked and ran her tongue under her teeth, not smiling.

"I missed it," Alex told her.

The vast appliance warehouse seemed to whirr with the dull hum of all its wares. First in the line of dispirited home-improvers stood a thin, wiry girl, whose scuffed jeans hung sagging on her hips, and whose uncertainty weighed down her rebellion.

"And I suppose you'll be wanting that delivered?" The suave, slick-haired blonde salesman handed Kelly a bundle of warranties, manuals and general notes on the science of air-conditioning.

"How much would that cost?" she asked, meek but determined. This piece of metal had just set her back one hundred-and-fifty dollars, and she didn't have a check coming until next Friday.

"Sixty," the clerk admitted, clearly displeased with this tactless question.

"Oh. No, I'll just take it. It's not far, really."

"If you're sure," he replied ominously.

The salesman carried the bulky box to the door of the warehouse for her, but somehow this gesture seemed an imposition rather than a favor. Kelly wanted only to be rid of him, to cope privately with her burden, without the snide oversight of this impersonal arm of the appliance industry.

She tried to take the crate from him after they'd passed through the doors, sure that here her rights to freedom and privacy would come into effect. He allowed her to do so, but didn't immediately return to his post inside, as she had hoped. Under the cumbersome mass of the box, Kelly squirmed and struggled, smaller even than her usual scrawny size. But only two streets, one-and-a-half avenues: Surely she could manage it that far, if he would only leave her alone. She was wasting inexpendable energy supporting the bulky crate as they stood here like this, but she couldn't begin to attempt to carry it away until he left her.

"I'll hail you a cab," he offered, and for an instant became not the depersonalized retailer, but a chivalrous young man looking out for a damsel about to be in some distress. However, the tone of his offer didn't suit this rosy image. Kelly noted the presumptuousness of it above all; he wasn't asking her whether she wanted a cab, but rather telling her he was going to put her in one. And he'd waited so long to do so, as if he'd silently won some argument with her by wearing her arms out this much longer. Her hands slipped and wrestled with the box. Feeling brattier than she should have at twenty-two, Kelly declined. At the moment, she didn't have the strength for maturity.

"No, thank you; I'll manage just fine without. It really isn't far."

But it was. By the time the man had finished off a now somewhat deflated round of 'Are you *sure*?'s and gone back inside, Kelly was shaking with the effort of standing, and she still had all those steps to make. About five blocks, the distance. That wasn't so far. But how, how, how many steps in each of those blocks. She couldn't go on, but her dignity didn't admit of the possibility of going back and saying she had changed her mind. Besides, if she did that, or if she tried to hail a cab herself, who would watch the air-conditioner for her? One didn't leave one-hundred-fifty dollar items lying unattended on the street, though she doubted that a thief in such case would be able to get away very quickly.

Yet even these idle excursions on which she tried to send her thoughts didn't succeed in distracting her from the impossible situation. She did succeed in displeasing each rushing passerby on the sidewalk, either by taking up more than her share of space, or by walking too slowly. Even shriveled old ladies with pushcarts on their way in and out of the neighboring supermarket seemed to speed by Kelly. It wasn't just the matter of her slow progress; it was the unachievable nature of the whole enterprise. Her strength had dropped away by large degrees since she'd first taken this monstrous box upon herself, and there was no question of her having enough left even to finish this block at the rate she was going. If she ever reached the corner of the street, she'd never make it across before the signal changed.

If only there were handles. That was the chief obstacle to her slogging through this grim labor. She had to hold her arms at an awkward and obtuse angle to support the box, and inevitably one of its fierce corners thrust into her stomach. The plastic cords strapped around the crate at first seemed the solution to this dilemma, but an attempt to exploit their positioning soon betrayed their uselessness. The air-conditioner was so heavy, and the cords so unyielding, that they chafed and scraped her palms into thick red lines of blisters before she could pull her fingers out from underneath.

There was no way around it; she couldn't go on any further. If she could only rest awhile, there might be a chance, but she couldn't take a dozen more steps without collapsing. At least she was no longer in front of the broad expanse of the appliance store; she felt that she'd escaped their jurisdiction at last, and was no longer subject to their better-knowing advice. She wished she could set her burden down completely out of sight of their warehouse, but this was not to be; she couldn't make it that much further. She edged her way to the exterior of the supermarket, dropped the weight she wasn't sure she'd be able to pick up again, and sat down on top of it. Only fair that it should bear her weight after forcing her to bear its.

Now the passersby weren't displeased with her, but rather looked on in sympathy for her trial. Nevertheless, none of them was moved to offer her aid. There was something innately disreputable about this small woman lugging a giant box down the street; why hadn't she had the thing delivered, or, if she were determined to transport it on her own, why didn't she have movers, friends, at the very least a taxi? Their judgment amounted to a condescending, if friendly, condemnation; she must have erred to come to such a pass, and now must sort it out as best as she could, the poor little thing.

After a time, Kelly—contrary to her own expectations—managed to raise the accursed carton back to its original height and begin walking again, but this pleasant surprise soon faded. She tired more quickly and more thoroughly than she had on the first trip. She barely made it to the dormitory on the other side of the grocery store before she had to take a seat on top of the box again, desperately searching for a solution. She'd have to call someone, that much was sure. But she felt a certain embarrassment at her self-inflicted crisis, and hesitated at each number she looked up in her phone. She was most inclined towards Angie. Angie lived in the apartment building not two blocks from where Kelly now sat marooned, and, after eight years of friendship, Angie dare not do a thing but understand.

But Angie was busy today. She'd said as much the evening before, when Kelly had remarked that she'd be moving today, and could use some help. Still, neither of them could have foreseen the urgent nature of the situation, and Kelly felt sure of Angie's aid, should she decide to call on her. It seemed so messy to call on outside help, though. Perhaps she could make it after all. Kelly gave an experimental tug at one of the plastic cords with an arm that felt permanently crooked, and decided that this wasn't the case.

A young man in a grocer's uniform, outside for a cigarette break, regarded her, unable to overcome his sense of chivalry.

"Do you need a hand with that?" he asked.

It was safe for a stranger to ask her that now; there was no longer anything especially incongruous in her appearance, for she sat outside of a dormitory, where, with her wrinkled t-shirt, thrift-shop jeans, and young face, she could just as easily have lived. There was nothing disreputable about resting an appliance on the ground, so long as one did so outside one's own residence.

"Oh, no thank you," Kelly replied almost in spite of herself. "I'm just waiting for someone."

She and the young man were greatly relieved to hear this. He hadn't had any desire to help her, and probably couldn't have left work long enough to do so. She wouldn't have wanted to have him come into her apartment, or to impose on a stranger to the extent that this would necessitate. Yet someone had had to make the offer, and it warmed the hearts of all the neighboring sidewalk-walkers to see that the poor girl might have help if she liked, and wasn't so poor after all.

It couldn't be helped now; she'd better get someone to come or she'd have lied to that young man just now. Well, it would have to be Angie. Everyone else was at work or the wrong person to ask. Surely this wasn't the most fun way for Angie to spend her day off work, but wasn't that what friends were for, making little sacrifices like this for one another? Kelly dialed Angie, who was apparently not so busy but that she could answer on the second ring.

"I'm *so* sorry," Kelly told her, letting her actual frustration and closeness to tears come into her voice, and then some. "I hate to ask you on your day off and I know you're busy and everything, but I don't know who else to call; I'm right across from you by those dorms, and I've got this terribly heavy air-conditioner I can't move from the spot."

"Oh, alright," Angie sighed, more amused than annoyed. "I'll be there in ten minutes. Just have to put my shoes on."

Kelly sat back on her box and waited. What a wonderful thing, to have such a reliable friend. How silly of her to think Angie would object to helping her out at a time like this. In a way it was fortuitous that she'd had to call Angie today; it reminded her of the upcoming Wednesday, when Angie would turn twenty-three. Kelly decided she needed to get Angie something extra-special now, not only because twenty-three was a rather anticlimactic birthday, but also because Kelly was happy to know someone like Angie, someone she could count on. She wanted to make Angie feel happy and appreciated. On top of which, she now felt that she owed Angie something.

Angie arrived in pomp and circumstance in spite of her uncharacteristically dowdy appearance. Though Kelly knew Angie didn't like to leave her apartment looking less than her best, here she was, already waving from the end of the block, hair un-straightened, clad in the fitted tank top and baggy sweat pants she wore around her home. She looked solid, athletic, capable. Kelly waved back, careful to look a little chagrinned and very much in need of assistance.

"Why didn't you have it delivered?" Angie demanded.

Kelly did her best to explain. The cost was reason enough, but she wanted to tell Angie how irritated she'd been by the attitude of the sleek blonde man and the company he represented.

"Oh, never mind," Angie cut her off. "I'll hail a cab."

Kelly agreed without a word.

"But that's only four blocks away," the cabby objected after they'd sweated and strained the box into the trunk of his taxi.

Kelly didn't know why he should object; what was it to him whether they paid him for a trip they didn't need? Perhaps he didn't think it worth his time to drive them there.

"The box is very heavy," she explained aloud.

Angie didn't offer to split the cab fare, which was fitting, but Kelly nevertheless made a great show of covering it for both of them.

"This one's on me." She waved away the money Angie hadn't taken out of her purse. "You are being such a big help to me."

The cabby, uncomprehending of their heavy burden from the beginning, soon sped off.

"Heave-ho!" Kelly tried for a laugh and the two lifted the box by the plastic straps, which, with the weight halved, weren't really so abrasive after all. She opened the door to her building, and they tugged the crate against its will into the lobby, where they allowed it respite at the foot of the stairs.

"Let's take a break," Kelly suggested. Angie might only have started, but she'd been at this too long already.

"Sure," Angie agreed, only too happy not to lift or carry. They stopped again at the top of the first flight.

"How about you push and I pull from above?" Angie offered. She put one hand on the wide curve of her hip as she made the suggestion, such that Kelly couldn't make the mistake of disobeying.

"Okay," Kelly agreed, though she felt that this was neither the most efficient way to move the box, nor the most equal to divide the labor. Of the latter she was even more convinced as her eyes teared up with the effort of putting herself beneath a weight which seemed determined to resist her. Angie, she noticed, had had the nerve to break quite a little sweat, as if she had any idea what the box really weighed. The illustrious puller-from-above was doing little more than getting in the way, as far as Kelly could see. But these were ungenerous thoughts; Angie didn't have to help at all, and got little benefit from doing so. Furthermore, Kelly could never have made it even this far without her help.

Kelly was shaking again by the time they reached the third floor, and now a fatigue too great even to allow her to rest in stillness had spread throughout her. Her whole body and especially her hands vibrated with small, nervous tremors, while her arms shook in broad, visible jerks.

Angie had a thick line of droplets along her upper lip, a comical round mustache, but was otherwise unperturbed. She gave her beneficiary a pat on the back so encouraging that Kelly could feel the force of it rattling back and forth from one of her thin shoulder-blades to the other.

"Come on," Angie invited Kelly heartily to the last flight. "Just one more!"

What was meant as a pep-talk sounded like a death knell to Kelly. She could not, could not, could not move from the spot, not yet; she would break into pieces if she had to lift that thing one more time, and especially if she tried to do it now. She only wanted just a little rest. Couldn't Angie see she was exhausted?

"Just let's wait a minute. Don't you want a break?"

"Hah! I could do this all day," Angie replied, with what was meant as a grin of camaraderie. "Now let's get this done."

Kelly realized that she really didn't understand, and sought another means of escape, another way to talk herself into a little more time.

"Yeah, I bet. I'll just run up now and unlock the door, and then we can make one big push and get it into the apartment."

"Great idea," Angie, impatient to be done with this chore, pretended to agree.

Kelly scrambled up the stairs with the false but lovely sensation that she could run away from the horrible burden, leave it behind with Angie, and never look back. As her shaking hands disrupted the placement of key in lock, Kelly allowed herself to revel in the absurd thought. She imagined especially that Angie would call after her, call to her to take the box back, but would eventually give up, and quietly accept the weighty curse as her own. As a third and fourth time Kelly's hands skipped away from their duty she really did hear Angie calling her, and she cursed instead of replying. The sweat of frustration joined that of fatigue and her eyes stung as makeup and moisturizer seeped toxic into them. Her eyes in turn poured forth their own kind of sweat, polluted water like tears but painful on its way out. She closed them, made her two hands one fist around the keys, and got her door open.

She turned out the bolt-lock to prop the door ajar, and walked, slow and steady now, down the all-too-short flight of stairs back to Angie, back to the once-promising addition to her household.

"Took you long enough." Angie laughed as she spoke to indicate the flippancy of her words, but Kelly knew that she did so only to avoid an open conflict. When Kelly didn't respond, Angie cocked her head in the direction of the air-conditioner. "Shall we?" she simpered, putting on a regal tone for no conceivable reason. Kelly wondered why she couldn't speak in her own voice, take responsibility for what she said.

The two stepped and stooped to pick up their burden again, but there was a small error in communication. Kelly and Angie only narrowly avoided colliding when each made a move for the pull-position on the box. A thin cloud of hostility rose from them like steam from ice cubes dropped in boiling water, but dissipated as quickly.

"Sorry," said Kelly. "I thought we'd switch places."

"Oh. I didn't know we were doing that." Angie meant her ignorance of the notion to be a rejection of it, but Kelly pretended not to notice.

"Yeah, let's. Just for this flight." Kelly added this qualifier as if it were a concession to Angie, but as there remained only the one flight, she wasn't doing her any favors. Angie couldn't come up with a valid reason to disagree, so she nodded and made a great show of getting beneath the heavy box. They made the slow, rocky ascent and Kelly noted to her satisfaction that, as she had imagined, pulling really was far easier than pushing, and further that, with Angie in the more difficult spot, this last couple dozen steps took much longer than the previous flights. Once they had mounted the last step, each relinquished her stiff hold on the box and shook out her arms from shoulders to fingers, trying to get them loose again. Both laughed when they noticed this.

"Damn," Angie observed none too keenly. "That thing is heavy."

Kelly agreed while they kicked and shoved the box over her threshold. Now that the horrible task was on the point of completion, she overflowed with triumph and affection for the friend who'd helped her achieve it. She felt as if the weight of the air-conditioner had sat all this time on her spirits, but had now been lifted off. How silly of her to allow her frustration with this chore to become resentment towards Angie. Angie, who was spending her day off...

Kelly began trying to think of subtle ways to find out exactly what Angie would like for her birthday. Just a gift wouldn't be enough; Kelly wanted to be sure that Angie would have a good time, a special day to more than make up for the one she'd sacrificed to this project. However, she realized that she'd lost her friend's latest remark in the jumble of her thoughts.

"What?"

"It's hot as hell in here," Angie repeated. "Whew!"

Kelly laughed and shook her head. She wouldn't have missed much if that comment had passed her by. While outside it'd been a seventy-something sort of weather, pleasant enough not to call attention to itself, the uncirculating humid air of her new apartment leapt at them, attacked them, the moment they stepped in the door.

"Yep," she told Angie, holding back as much of the snideness in her tone as she could. "That's why I bought this."

Kelly patted the cardboard box, whose contents responded with a dull metal thud. No longer did she regret her purchase, now that she stood to be rid of this too-tropical indoor atmosphere. She thought of the last week there, the sweat that she could wash off in the shower but never really be rid of. She took a deep breath of swampy air and savored its unpleasantness. The two friends stood wrapped in separate swaths of thought, but Angie's fell away more quickly.

"Can't you open a window or something? This is disgusting. Look at me. I'm sweating like a pig."

Obediently, Kelly both opened a window, and looked at Angie, whose plain grey tank was now decorated with damp thick lines, one below each armpit, two on her stomach, another below her expansive breasts. The heat of the room bred a haziness of thought, and Kelly found herself spending a few seconds wondering whether pigs really sweated as much as everyone thought, before she came up with something rational to say.

"Do you want to sit down?" she asked Angie when a weak and sickly breeze had begun to squirm in from the airshaft that the living room window looked out on.

They took a seat on the clunky black sofa opposite the window. The slick leather glued itself to the skin of all four thighs on it, regardless of any intervening cotton. Kelly and Angie took off their shoes. They looked out at the windows of the neighboring apartments. Some windows had AC units installed at the top, and others at the bottom on the sill, but every window had an air-conditioner in it. Resentment flickered over Kelly, until she recalled that soon, she too, might proudly show off her appliance, though she planned to put the air-conditioner in her bedroom. It would be good to have some fresh air while she slept. This last thought was so delightful that she wanted to hug everyone and everything in the room. Instead, she began to tell Angie about the man at the appliance store, transforming him into a veritable monster of smugness and insincerity, though if he'd been present at the moment, she might have hugged him, too. In spite of Kelly's delight, she had to admit that it was too hot to hug anyone, and so satisfied herself by trying to relate the morning's uninspiring events to her friend.

She worried that her story was dull and pointless, but was pleased to see an animated look of interest on Angie's face. There was truly nothing in the world like a close friend, one who would listen to you ramble on about anything, and who wouldn't feel disgusted by the visible marks of sweat you left on the leather furniture. One who would sit and talk in your humid, stifling apartment, and not complain. Kelly watched Angie's face and pictured a look of happy surprise coming onto it. Maybe she would send Angie flowers at her office on Wednesday. Roses, of course. Pink or red, something showy. The reception desk was at the front of the office, so everyone who worked there would see them delivered to Angie and envy her. Kelly knew that would please Angie most, since, loud and forceful as Angie's presence was, it was unlikely that any of her more elite coworkers would remember her birthday.

"What was I saying?" she asked Angie, realizing that she'd trailed off somewhere and never found her way back.

"Who knows?" Angie gave a cheerful shrug of her broad, round shoulders. "Are you gonna turn that on, or what?"

"What?" Kelly followed Angie's eyes in the direction of the box they'd stranded by the door. "Oh. Sure. Of course. But I think we need to install it or something."

"Even just to put it on for a few minutes?" Angie groaned. "Couldn't we just plug it in out here to make sure it works?"

Kelly sighed and opened the box. She knew Angie. There was no use in arguing. Kelly didn't have the energy to lift the unit out of the box, so she simply tore the thick cardboard case away from it, as if peeling some large post-industrial fruit. Once inside, she paused to regard the whole of it. There were pages and pages of instructions, not just in one booklet but many. Some were about maintenance, some about installation. One was a catalogue of replaceable parts. Still another dealt with questions of insurance. This unit came with a comprehensive warranty: If the company couldn't repair it, they would replace it. This guarantee did little to reassure Kelly. Far from needing a second unit, she was having enough trouble doing anything with the first one.

Bewildered, Kelly forgot that she'd been looking for the cord to plug the air-conditioner in, and instead began to sift through all the unapproachable packets of words. Even when she took the time to focus on an individual sentence, she could make no sense of it: "In case of Storm Window or Wooden Sill be sure to install Flanges in perpendiculated accordance with Left and Right Window Panel Strips," read one. "See figure B6.1."

Angie sat waiting with only the damp imprint of Kelly for company. She drummed her fingers on the arm of the sofa, but this made next to no noise, so she cleared her throat and tapped the heel of one foot on the wooden floor. Kelly didn't appear to notice.

"What's the hold-up?" Angie asked her. "Just plug it in."

"It's so confusing," Kelly called back to her, her voice small and lost across even the short distance from hall to living room.

Angie uncrossed her legs and crossed them in the opposite direction. She took the elastic hair tie off her wrist and tried to put her hair up neatly. By tilting her head, she could make out a faint reflection on the half-raised window. She tapped her fingers and her heels in rhythm. She didn't understand how plugging in an appliance could be confusing, but when Kelly gave no further clarification, Angie sighed, tore herself off the sofa like an old Band-Aid, and went to check on her friend.

"Did you need a hand?" Angie could see the electric cord and the three-pronged plug. She could also see the three-pronged electrical outlet on the wall. She could not see what the problem was.

"I can't tell the English directions from the Spanish ones," Kelly told her. "And these illustrations…"

Kelly couldn't summon the energy to try and describe them. Instead, she thrust one such packet of diagrams towards Angie. Angie didn't take it. She reached around the thin form crouched over the air-conditioner and connected the appliance to the wall. She knelt next to Kelly and pressed the power button. The machine groaned itself alive, its whirr joining the distant hum of its brethren outside the living room window.

"That was real hard. Not." Angie smirked at Kelly, wanting gratitude, or at least admiration.

"But we can't just leave it here. It has to go in the window."

"Says who?"

In answer Kelly merely shoved the pile of papers at her again, relying on their authority as if the manufacturer had specialized in holy writ.

"Okay, okay." Angie took them this time, but only glanced at them. "I'll help you put it in right, but let's leave it on while we figure out how to do it. Can't hurt, right?"

Angie's entry into the installation process breezed refreshingly into Kelly's tension as the cooler air of the shaftway drifted through the room. She no longer felt helpless. Surely between the two of them, they could understand it, at least make enough sense of it to get by. Hope filled her again. She hadn't thought Angie would stay past dropping off the crate. Kelly thought of throwing Angie a surprise party in the new apartment. Nothing extravagant, just cocktails, cake, a few friends. With the air-conditioning on, it wouldn't be oppressive even to have a dozen or so people in the room, though it might still feel overcrowded. Kelly thought of ways she could trick Angie into coming over without spoiling the surprise. Perhaps she would feign relationship trouble, and rely on that to draw her sympathetic friend over. Angie wouldn't refuse to talk her through a breakup any more than she'd refused to help her with this minor crisis. Then Angie's and Kelly's friends would spring out and Angie would giggle and glow with joy, probably make some bad joke about wondering what the occasion was.

The two women and the installation manual returned to the sofa. In silence Angie and Kelly both read or pretended to read the directions over and over again.

"Are you getting this?" Angie asked after they had thus occupied ten or fifteen minutes.

"I can't look at it anymore." Kelly shook her head, her frustration now physical, a dizzy headache and an inability to breathe in deeply enough. "Let's take out the pieces and maybe we'll be able to tell how they go together."

"I don't know if that's the best idea."

Kelly guessed that Angie only objected out of reluctance to move the air-conditioner from its current position. She met this objection accordingly, as if Angie had spoken it aloud.

"Look, it's not even working." Kelly waved her hand in the thick hot air as if to sweep some of it in Angie's direction, and so prove her point.

"You have to give it time."

Kelly wondered where Angie had gotten that authoritative tone. It wasn't as if she could understand the instructions any better than Kelly could.

"I don't think so. If anything, it's hotter in here than before."

"That's crazy." But as the two got up from the sofa and walked towards the air-conditioning unit, they could feel the dry, hot air coming from it. Kelly stepped closer to the machine, hands out, feeling the weak flow of cool from one side, and the rush of overwhelming heat from the other. She put her foot down next to the unit, and then quickly jumped back, the cold water already soaking into her white socks.

"Shit." She rushed to pull the plug on the whirring mess and then to save the papers that appeared pertinent from the spreading puddle beneath it. "That's why it has to go in the window."

Wordless, Angie got a roll of paper towels from the kitchen and dropped sheet after sheet into the flood. She kept her head bent and solemn, the picture of a noble-minded martyr suffering for her cause.

"Forget it," Kelly told her. "Just help me carry this to my bedroom."

"Don't worry," Angie replied. "If anything happened to it, we're well within the thirty-day warranty."

Kelly had nothing to say to that.

Though the air-conditioner, without its cardboard case and now wet, had become slippery, carrying it from the front hall to Kelly's bedroom was not a fraction of the labor that getting it into her apartment had been. After a second trip to the hall, Angie and Kelly began opening small plastic baggies and prying apart Styrofoam casings. Metal frame-pieces, rolled-up strips of insulation foam, washers, bolts, screws and accordion-folded plastic panels crowded Kelly's floor. She went to look for a screwdriver in the travel-sized toolkit her father had given her as a housewarming gift. She brought back a Philips and a flathead; she felt that they'd need both of these and more. Back on her bedroom floor, she found Angie with the instructions unfolded once more.

"They're actually easier to understand in French," she informed Kelly.

"You're just showing off," Kelly scoffed, then she reconsidered. "How do you say 'Flange' in French?"

"What? Oh. I don't know. It just says 'Flange' again. I guess it doesn't translate."

"Well I want to know what the hell a Flange is." Kelly disliked the shape of the word as she spoke it. It had a sneaky, dangerous sound. Like something whose predominant action was lurking.

None of the large and small pieces on her floor looked ominous enough to be a Flange. In the black-and-white picture showing the installation of the Flanges, she couldn't tell which part was which.

"So look it up," was Angie's suggestion.

"It's probably not even a real word." Kelly let the issue fade, pretending to concentrate on the construction of the frame. It wasn't merely the effort of finding her dictionary and flipping through it, nor even Angie's self-congratulating tone, that stopped her. She didn't feel that her vocabulary would benefit from the addition of the word.

Kelly worked on assembling the Left Filler Panel while Angie put together the right one. Together they fitted them into the Window Frame. They didn't speak, outside of Angie's occasional remark on the heat that Kelly no longer noticed. At length it seemed all that was left was to fit the Right and Left Window Sashes into the Window Frame, and then put the whole affair into the window with the AC unit. There were a great deal of screws, bolts and locks left over which neither could think where to place, but there was nothing Kelly thought could be described as a Flange.

Kelly pushed the thick glass window open. There was no screen. She blew a dusty anemic spider web out of the way and leaned out. The sky was an irregular rectangle of blue, framed by the upper floors of the cluster of apartment buildings. Far below, the cement bottom of the air shaft was coated in aluminum siding and various pieces of litter which no one cared to retrieve. Not that they would've been able to. Kelly wondered whether anyone ever cleaned it out. Someone must, or the cigarette butts alone would have reached to her window by now. Everywhere between cement floor and sky were whirring, dripping air-conditioners. She picked up the metal frame and adjusted its width to fit the window.

"Here, I'll hold that in place," Angie offered, "if you'll just pick up the AC and put it in." She tensed the muscles in her upper arms and leaned at an awkward angle over Kelly's bed to hold the frame, as if hers were the real physical undertaking involved.

"Sure." Kelly bent and got her hands around the sides of the unit. Her blistered fingers trembled again, as if in trained reaction to their placement there. She was relieved, however, to have come so far that only this mindless physical task remained. At least she didn't have to look at the manual anymore. She'd begun to feel as if her brain, like her other muscles, were jerking and twitching with overexertion. Her headache hadn't gone away, but merely hung in the background, an atmosphere as heavy as the heat of the room. It felt good to have the window open, but she couldn't avoid the feeling that she was only taking in everyone else's refuse, breathing in the air that the other air-conditioners had expelled into the shaftway. Kelly inhaled with her mouth closed as she lifted the appliance.

"Easy does it," Angie urged as Kelly propped the machine on the window sill, still holding it. Kelly wondered why her friend had found the phrase necessary. She imagined Angie hoped to establish a false impression of helpfulness.

"Okay, now just push it into the frame," Angie advised Kelly. But there was no getting the air-conditioner into the frame; that much quickly became apparent. While Kelly estimated that the frame would fit perfectly around the indented strip in the middle of the unit, the manufacturers had clearly intended that the frame and the air-conditioner should go into the window together, already attached. Otherwise it was impossible either to get the AC unit into the frame, or to adjust the accordion-folding panels to the width of the window. Angie and Kelly, each still holding her charge in place, stared at the impossibility as if it would soon disappear.

"Oh, shit," Kelly remarked.

"Oh, Flange," Angie seconded her. They both laughed. Again Angie assumed control of the situation.

"So you just pull it off of the ledge and hold it, and then I'll fit the frame around it, and we can push it in."

"I can't," Kelly protested. "I can't hold it any longer." Even with most of its weight supported by the window sill, the air-conditioner was fast becoming unmanageable. Kelly thought she might lose it altogether if she tried to take more of its weight onto herself. She thought of the air-conditioner falling onto her hard wooden floor after all this. She wondered whether it would break.

She thought of the air-conditioner falling onto one of her feet. She felt certain that it would break.

"You're holding it right now."

Kelly saw that there was no way out. "Okay, but hold it for one second."

Angie raised her eyebrows and took the frame out of the window. She set it on the black sheets of Kelly's bed, where it left a stark outline of pale grey dust. She took the AC unit from Kelly. Kelly wiped her damp, slippery hands on the thighs of her jeans. Their first contact left two clear dark palm prints. Kelly hoped that Angie didn't notice, but knew that she did. It didn't matter. Kelly put her hands on the AC unit next to Angie's. She nodded. Angie took her hands away. Kelly locked her fingers to keep them from trembling. Angie referred to the instructions, set them down, and then referred to them again. Kelly could feel every line on her palms by the seeping moisture soaking through each one. The sweat stung her blisters. Angie began unscrewing the accordion panel from the left side of the frame.

"What are you doing?" Kelly wanted to know.

"It says we shouldn't have put these in yet."

"Are you sure?" Kelly pressed down with the tips of her fingers, trying to get a better grip on the unit, but its hard metal surface pushed against her fingernails, seemed to repel them. Angie set the screwdriver on the window sill, and the frame back on the bed. The rectangles of dust it left overlapped each other like a squared-off Venn diagram. Angie perused the manual again, entirely at her leisure.

"Oh, no. You're right." Angie continued to page through the instructions.

Kelly wanted to scream at her, or just at the unbearableness of the weight she was supporting. Instead, she forced her voice into a friendly, bantering tone.

"Angie, you've got to take over. I can't hold the Flanging thing a minute longer." The joke was getting tired now, but the two of them laughed for old time's sake. Angie cracked her knuckles. Kelly cringed, tried to hide her disgust, and then her growing resentment, as Angie deliberately popped the joint on each finger, and then the thumbs, too.

"That gives you arthritis, you know," she told Angie.

"That's an old wives' tale." Angie put her hands on the unit besides Kelly's. "You can let go; I've got it."

Kelly took her hands away. She wiped them on her jeans again, picked up the directions and tried to figure out what to do next. She knew she had to appear busy. She looked first at the words, and then at the pictures, trying to get an idea of the whole process. She didn't want to admit that she couldn't understand either.

"Take your time," Angie said, faking a laugh.

Kelly wanted to tell her that she'd taken infinitely longer herself, and still accomplished nothing, but she kept the thought to herself. This and the other bitten-back frustrations of the day swarmed about inside her like a pile of wriggling maggots. She imagined them evolving, growing, breeding.

Kelly picked up the window frame from the bed, hiding a frown as she noted the mess left behind. She'd just washed her linens the day before. She picked up the accordion panel Angie had removed and left on the floor, and began screwing it back into place. She couldn't think, and wondered whether some fresh air might help dissolve her headache. After giving the final turn to the screw, she lowered her arms, still holding the frame, and put her head out the window. She breathed and breathed the air. It felt cleaner than that inside her room, but not much cooler. She had a vision of herself flying away out the window, leaving Angie and the AC unit behind. Perhaps the air-conditioner would be installed when she came back, though she thought not.

"What are you doing?" Angie demanded. "I'm killing myself here." She didn't play the remark off as a joke, and Kelly felt alarmed. She feared the opening of hostilities between them, feared the kinds of things she might say if they started snapping at each other. She pictured a cloud of stinging insects flying out of her mouth and settling on Angie.

"Sorry. I needed some air."

"Yeah, well I do, too, but you don't see me dropping everything to go breathe." Kelly didn't bite her tongue at this remark, but she felt it push against her tightly clenched teeth, an unwilling prisoner.

"Sorry," Kelly repeated when she felt that she could safely say the word, and nothing more. She unscrewed the screws in the middle of the frame, and separated the two halves of it. She put the first one around the AC unit, and then slipped the other one into place, fitting them into each other. She picked up the screwdriver and screws. Carefully, she screwed the bottom screw into place, then started on the top one.

"I'll do that."

"What?" Kelly looked up.

"You've had your break now. You hold it for a while and I'll screw that in."

"Could we just set it down for a minute?" Kelly asked, knowing Angie would find some reason to say no. "Why does one of us have to hold it?"

"If you think you'll be able to pick it back up, I can put it down now, but I certainly won't be lifting that thing again."

"Fine. You're right. I'll hold it." Kelly wanted to make some cutting witticism but couldn't come up with one. She satisfied herself with the thought that she was taking the high road, keeping her irritation inside. She put her hands on the unit next to Angie's.

"Ready?" Angie asked.

"Ready." Kelly delivered the word as coldly as she could. Her fingers felt as if they were all being bent backwards. Angie picked up the screwdriver and tightened the last screw. She set the screwdriver on the sill, and stepped back as if to admire her craftsmanship.

"Okay," Kelly reminded her. "Now we have to get it installed in the window."

"Yeah. You just push it in slowly and I'll lower the window until it fits."

Kelly noticed once more how Angie always took it for granted that the lighter task should fall to her. It wasn't as if Angie were delicate. Ordinarily Kelly would've dismissed such an unkind thought, but she no longer saw the point. She wanted to object but couldn't see how.

Kelly shifted the unit further out onto the sill, trying to let the window frame bear some of the weight. The air-conditioner wouldn't balance on its own, and she had to hold onto it as tightly as ever. Angie lowered the window a few tenths of an inch at a time. When it was within a fingertip's distance of the air-conditioner, she had to push it open again so Kelly could angle the indentation of the unit to line up with the edge of the window. While Kelly held the unit at the correct angle, Angie took the opportunity to line up the folding panels on either side of it. Kelly felt her hands grow more slippery than ever, and still there was nothing to dig her nails into.

"Come on, you can do that after," she told Angie. "Just get the window down so I don't have to hold this up anymore."

"Gosh, hold your horses a second. I gotta do this first." Angie made still more languid motions with her fingers to get the side panels in place. Kelly didn't believe that the side panels needed to be fitted before the window could be closed. As always with Angie, this was an issue of winning the argument, having the last word.

"Angie, I honestly can't hold this up. If you're going to take this long then you're going to have to hold it, and I'll do the sides. I literally cannot do this a second longer or my hands are going to fall off."

"Wow, drama queen much?"

Angie cracked the knuckle of each index finger. Kelly didn't bother to hide her revulsion, but only waited for Angie to reach her hands to the unit so she could pull hers away. Free of the metal weight, Kelly reached and pushed down on the top of the window, but something wasn't right. Rather than completing the couple inches of distance between its initial height and where the air-conditioner should have been, the window slammed against the wooden sill with a bang that jolted Kelly up to her elbows. She couldn't understand where the bone-jarring sensation came from, or where her air-conditioner had gone. Angie stared blankly at the closed window. Kelly shrieked.

"Hey, calm down. Just calm down, alright?" Angie put a moist heavy palm on one of Kelly's narrow shoulders, which Kelly shook off.

"You were supposed to have it!" Kelly shouted, and kept shouting.

"Would you shut up!" Angie yelled back when Kelly's wailing threatened to drag on indefinitely. Out of habit, Kelly obeyed.

Angie stepped over to the window, picked up the three-pronged plug hanging into the room. She pressed her damp forehead against the glass to look straight down, then smiled.

"We didn't lose it. You're sitting there screaming your head off, and we didn't even lose it. Look—"Angie beckoned Kelly closer. Kelly pressed her face next to the smudge of sweat Angie's had left, and looked down. Her air-conditioner hadn't plunged as far as she'd imagined. The tenants in the apartment below had installed their own larger, more powerful unit at the top of their window, and this sturdier appliance had caught Kelly's before it could descend more than a few feet. It sat there now, partly held up by the taut cord, but mostly resting on the other unit.

"See?" Angie said. "All we have to do is pull it up. Now you just hold the plug and I'll open—"

"No," Kelly cut her off. "You hold the plug. And try actually holding onto it this time."

"I wasn't ready. Did you hear me say I was ready? You shouldn't have let go so quickly!"

Kelly ignored Angie's words, and simply waited for her to clasp both her hands around the end of the wire.

"Are you ready this time?" she asked after a minute or two.

"Of course I'm ready. Open the damned window."

Kelly waited another half a minute before raising the window.

"I just wanted to make sure," she said, "that you were ready."

After she'd opened the window, Kelly stepped to one side to be sure that Angie had room to haul the prize back into the room. She didn't want to get in the way, and furthermore, she didn't want Angie to be able to blame her if they messed something else up. Kelly watched Angie's hands on the wire. They didn't move much. Angie gave a slow pull towards herself and the wire grew tight, a straight line from her hands to the air shaft. On her second pull, it grew tighter still. Kelly wanted to ask if the air-conditioner were close to coming up, but she kept quiet. On the third pull, Angie wrapped some of her end of the cord around her hands to keep it tight. The wire stretched to a straighter line than ever, then became a loose squiggle. Angie staggered back against Kelly's bed, no longer attached to anything. She looked at her hands, at the cord wrapped around them. She pulled the rest of the cord to herself. It came easily now, finally ending in a jagged rubber ring, a few colorful copper twists protruding in different directions from the tear.

Kelly looked at Angie and at both ends of the wire. She got up and walked over to the window. She looked out at the other air conditioners dripping water down the airshaft. She listened to them humming. Looking straight down, she now saw only a slight dent on top of the AC unit of the apartment below. She looked at the cement floor of the shaftway, at the brand new pile of junk metal there. Pictured Angie falling.

"It's not my fault!" Angie shouted. "It just broke."

Kelly looked at Angie, at the latest tide of sweat washing over her face. She didn't say anything. She looked at the open window and then at Angie again.

"Hey, this was my day off. I didn't have to come help you."

In silence, Kelly watched Angie speak. She looked puzzled, as if she didn't understand Angie's words, or even recognize them as such.

"Whatever. It wasn't my fault. It was as much your fault as it was mine." Angie didn't elaborate on how this was so. "Look, I'll even call the company for you, okay? It's under warranty, so don't get all freaked out about it. I'm sorry, okay? I'll pay for it if they won't. Do you hear me? Are you listening to what I'm saying?"

Kelly watched Angie. Angie was another diagram from the manual, a meaningless picture accompanied by equally meaningless words.

"You know what? I have a lot of other things to do today," Angie told Kelly. "I didn't have to come help you in the first place."

Kelly watched Angie leave.

The slick blonde salesman came the next day with the replacement unit. He was perspiring a little from the four flights, but not enough to dilute the crisp layer of gel coating his hair. He set the crate down on the floor of Kelly's bedroom. Kelly showed him the wreckage on the ground so far down the shaftway, and he nodded. Without being asked, he bent to open the box and began taking out the parts. He found the screwdriver on the sill where Angie had left it, and set about fitting together the various pieces. He worked automatically, without a visible thought or a glance at the manual. He must have done it a thousand times. Kelly knew he wasn't supposed to do anything but drop off her replacement, but she didn't thank him. She sat down on the edge of her bed and watched him at his task. When he had everything in its place, he brushed his hands across each other a few times, then used one of them to smooth his hair. He was sweating more than he had carrying the crate up the stairs. Kelly watched him and didn't speak. He plugged in the air-conditioner and turned it on.

"For future reference," he told her, "we offer installation with all of our delivery packages."

Kelly didn't reply or rise to show him out. But after the door had closed behind him, she got up and walked over to her desk. She picked up a ballpoint pen and opened her planner. She turned to the following Wednesday and drew three thin black lines through her last entry for the date. Kelly smiled to herself. Already an undercurrent of cool, clean air ran through the room.

Over

In a cramped or cozy kitchen in residential New Jersey, a lanky young man stood over a sinkful of dishes, passing each one he washed to the woman seated on the counter next to him to dry. They worked in angry silence. It was the end of an era.

The dishes clattered against each other in the sink. Ben, usually as gentle as the boyish face under his overgrown brown hair suggested, seemed almost determined to break some unsuspecting glass or plate. Molly put the last mug he'd handed her into the cabinet, then took it out again.

"This one isn't clean." She handed the mug back to Ben, who set down the pot he'd been scrubbing.

"What's wrong, Molly?" The two of them began to suspect that they weren't just talking about dishes anymore.

"You didn't rinse it when you put it in the sink. It has a stain on the rim." Molly spoke in a bland tone that belied her quiet triumph: Ben had failed again.

"Why is that automatically my fault?" he wanted to know. "How do we know it was me who didn't rinse?" Defeated before Molly replied, Ben put aside the pot. He wiped his hands on the front of his jeans and ran a palm across his forehead, although he wasn't working hard enough to perspire.

"I don't drink coffee, Ben, and you do. It's clearly a coffee stain. Besides, it doesn't matter who left it in the sink. You're washing and it's your job to make sure you get the dishes clean. It's disgusting to put dirty dishes in the cabinet with clean ones." She bit back a sigh after delivering this sermon; she hated the smug sound of her voice, but couldn't hold it in. Her only excuse was that he brought out her worst side.

"Sorry. Do you want to wash?"

"No, I don't want to, but I'll do it if you can't. Honestly, Benny. You're twenty-six years old. When are you going to grow up?"

"You're twenty-five and you don't know how to take turns. I always wash pretty much the whole sink while you sit there drying and complaining."

Molly slid off of the counter. Her weight—not heavy, but somewhat north of slender for her height—made a dull clank as she landed on the tile floor.

"Okay, Benny, we'll pretend this is kindergarten, and practice taking turns. I guess you want to call that your turn?" She gestured at the soapy mug Ben had unwittingly continued to polish.

"By all means—" He snatched the mug away as if she would try to steal it from him. "Let me finish this one. Heaven forbid that a dirty dish should make it into our spotless cabinet." Ben rinsed the mug with showy solicitude before passing it on to Molly. She drummed her fingers on the thick plastic edge of the countertop, as if the wait between dishes were really more than she could bear. She rattled about in the first two cluttered shelves for a spot to set the mug.

"Here, let me get that. The top shelf is practically empty." Ben spoke with genuine concern, though whether for Molly or for their collection of dishes was unclear. He stepped around her, demonstrating incontrovertibly his ability to reach the top of the cluttered wooden cabinet. Molly, given a choice between battle and truce, chose the former, and took this underscoring of their difference in height as a personal affront.

"I can reach perfectly fine," she snapped, again wanting to slap herself for her inability to just play nice. Straining onto the tips of her toes, she managed to push the mug over the edge of the top shelf. Ben frowned and ran a dishrag over the pot he'd left off on. He reached over Molly's head to display the ease with which he might set any dish he liked on the highest level of their cabinet.

"Damn it, Ben, can't you do anything right?" A look of murder appeared on Molly's round, freckled face. Ben couldn't guess what he'd done wrong this time.

"You got soap and water all over me." Molly pointed to a few drops that had landed on her neat red-orange braid and the pale rose blouse she wore out of spite for the laws of fashion.

"Sorry," Ben said again. "It was an accident."

"Well, it wouldn't have happened if the dish were actually dry. Can't you get anything right?" Once on the attack, Molly couldn't resist venting a few only tenuously related frustrations. "You know, I don't just throw anything on like you do. Some of us care how we look, and now you've ruined my favorite shirt."

Ben marveled at the coincidence that the particular shirt on which he'd inflicted such severe damages should happen to be Molly's favorite.

"It'll dry," he suggested, still willing to remain neutral, despite the slight Molly had thrown at his appearance. He looked down at the faded green t-shirt he was wearing, complete with coffee stain and unraveling hem. He hadn't thought it mattered so much how he dressed at home.

"It'll be one-up on the dishes if it does get dry." Molly gave the pot, which she could barely reach, a shove meant to imply that Ben hadn't put it into the cabinet correctly. Rather than adjusting the pot's position, however, she caused the hotly disputed mug to abandon hope and hurl itself out of the cabinet. Somehow the ceramic shattering on the floor made Molly angrier at Ben; she felt as if he'd caused her clumsiness.

"Let's just not talk anymore until we get this done, Molly. There's only a few dishes left." Ben's forgive-and-forget tone made Molly furious. His kindness seemed designed to make her feel guilty.

"Ah, Ben's big solution to everything: Just don't mention it. Well, that's fine by me." The wordless hostility resumed and the dishes found their way home, as clean and dry as they could reasonably expect under the circumstances. When she'd finished the last spoon, Molly disappeared into their bedroom and firmly shut the door. Ben swept up the pieces of the broken dish and followed her.

"Can I get my guitar out of there?" he asked through the closed door. A few months ago, before Molly had moved in, he might not have believed he'd end up knocking this timidly at his own door. No response reached him.

"Molly? Can I come in and get my guitar?" Nothing.

"Molly?" Maybe she'd fallen asleep or taken an important phone call, and couldn't answer. Ben turned the knob and entered. Molly, lying on her stomach in the middle of their bed, barely looked up from the magazine she was paging through.

"Are you okay, Molly?" Ben asked. "Didn't you hear me knocking?" He picked up his black guitar case, wanting to be ready to vacate the premises should it become dangerous to remain. Molly turned a page of her magazine, ostensibly unaware of Ben.

"Molly? Molly!" Ben set his guitar by the door and ran to Molly's side. Unwilling as he was to be a ghost in his own home, he feared that something might really be the matter. Molly had looked tired lately, with circles under her eyes and her face a little paler than usual.

She set down her magazine with an unconcerned calm.

"Yes?" she asked, as if answering a phone call from a telemarketer.

"I asked if you were okay. Why didn't you answer me?" Ben's concern faded into the beginnings of irritation.

"I'm sorry, Ben; I didn't know when you would be ready to stop playing the no-talking game. It's pretty hard to keep track of."

Ben and his guitar left the room without another word. After the door had closed behind them, Molly swore at herself and Ben under her breath. She tried to resume her reading, but ended up tossing the magazine to the floor. Much as she would've liked to be wrong just this once, she and Ben were going nowhere at a steady clip, and she knew she'd have to deal with it sooner or later. She knew that she, and not Ben, would have to deal with it, because Ben wasn't the kind who dealt with things. He always wanted to be nice and hope for the best, and Molly had loved that about him, but they weren't making it as a couple. Molly heard Ben busy with his pick and strings in the living room, and knew she needed to act now, before she could talk herself out of it and while she couldn't see the look on Ben's face.

In the living room Ben plucked at his acoustic guitar until his fingers hurt and after, trying to drown out thoughts he was afraid to think. He didn't want to believe, and ultimately couldn't, that he and Molly could fail. He played on, tried not to ask himself whether there was any way this could be the same Molly he'd met eighteen months before, the Molly he hadn't deserved but had gotten anyway, and now stood to lose. Molly had been the friend of a friend of a friend and so on in that direction, whom Ben met by pure chance at a rather lame party, post-college and pre-career. She'd looked out of place in the best of ways, as if the people and the scene around her were unworthy to touch her.

Starting a new song, Ben wondered what Molly had been up to in their room for so long. He paused to listen, but heard only routine noises: drawers opening and closing, the rustling of papers. He recalled asking Molly to move in with him. The season had been springtime and the proposition uncertain. Ben had packed a picnic lunch and driven Molly out to the Palisades to impress her with a view more glorious than his own romance could offer, but, in apt April fashion, it had rained the whole day, and they never left the car.

"You make this all worthwhile," he'd told her, and when she so shockingly descended into the realm of his domestic life, he'd believed she would keep on doing just that. Ben had remembered that grey afternoon, huddled up under their picnic blanket watching water hit the windshield, almost every day since. Without a view of the river or the city beyond the cliffs, he'd had the strangely pleasant sensation of drowning in Molly and the moment. He contemplated it now, and considered everything that had gone wrong since, from Molly's special way of making him feel unworthy, to that ceramic coffee mug hitting the floor. By the time he packed up his guitar, he felt ready to apologize for everything, so long as he could have some of that old Molly back again. It was probably his fault anyway.

Molly appeared in the hall as Ben left the living room, and they met each other halfway. Ben, relieved to have overcome his bad feelings at the same time Molly had hers, readied himself to say whatever she wanted to hear, but then realized that she hadn't come to apologize, was still unavailable. Perching a cordless phone between her ear and her shoulder, Molly juggled the weight of a plastic storage crate, usually shoved under the bed, from one arm to the other. Ben dropped his guitar and stepped out of her way, staring.

"Fifteen minutes." Molly set the crate by the front door, hung up the phone, and regarded Ben. In the box he saw her worn stuffed dog, a pile of clothing and shoes, and their bedside lamp.

"Spring cleaning?" he asked, with a desperate imitation of humor.

"It's July, Ben. I'm leaving."

"What do you mean?" He rushed to step between her and their bedroom, which it appeared he would soon have the misfortune of having to himself again.

"Excuse me." Molly stepped around Ben as if he'd gotten in her way only by accident. He watched in amazement as she produced load after load of her possessions, things he'd come to regard as part and parcel of a shared sense of home.

"Can we talk, Molly?" he pleaded after she'd brought out the last hastily packed shopping bag and sat down on the plastic crate to wait. "Where are you going?"

"Carly's picking me up."

"Can we talk about why you're leaving?" Ben moved to lean against the front door, the better both to be close to Molly, and to thwart her exit. Molly rose as he approached and began bustling about the living room, checking to make sure she hadn't forgotten anything. Ben sank into a seated position.

"Let's not kid ourselves, Ben. We can't stand each other."

"I can stand you, Molly. I love you."

Molly pretended to look for something under the sofa.

"Please don't do that."

"Do what?"

"That. Drive me up a wall for weeks and then think you can tell me you love me and make it all okay again. It's time we both moved on, so please don't even try it." The way Molly pronounced the word 'please' cut into Ben; he hated the implication that he would tell her he loved her to manipulate her.

"We can fix this, Molly. It isn't perfect, but I swear I'll make it better. Tell me what you need me to change and I'll do it. Really, I will." The note of groveling in Ben's voice, rather than ingratiating him to Molly, left her disgusted.

"There's nothing you can do," Molly snarled at Ben and the weak part of herself that wanted to believe they could get along again. "It's over. I can't stay here another minute, let alone live here. I don't want to see you anymore."

Someone knocked on the outside of the door, and Molly pulled it open, in spite of Ben's bulk in front of it. She greeted Carly with a tight smile. Ben seized the opportunity and one of Molly's legs, latching onto her like a toddler with abandonment issues.

"Don't leave me, Molly. I need you here with me. Promise me I'll see you again—I can change!"

"Can't you see I'm sick of you begging like a dog? Be a man!" Molly kicked herself free of his grasp. "Help me out, Carly." The two women began unloading Molly's presence from the flat. Ben, helpless even to try and slow them down, sank further onto the floor. He couldn't find the energy to feel ashamed as he whimpered and snuffled onto the linoleum.

Both women were relieved to leave him behind. Carly had expected a situation more passionately angry than painfully awkward, and she almost balked at the sight of Ben clinging to Molly. She had friends in common with Ben and might have refused to get involved if Molly hadn't sounded like she needed the help that badly.

As Molly lugged her bags and boxes down to the minivan, she repeated in her head the phrase 'clean break,' a rallying cry for the decision she was anything but sure of. Her steps and the words mirrored the rhythm of a light and dismal rain.

"I'll wait for you forever, Molly," Ben sobbed when she came for the last box. "It can't be over, not just like that."

In front of the building, Carly had started the car, the sooner to get them both out of there. 'Clean break, clean break,' Molly told herself, trying not to hear Ben as she hurried downstairs. She shoved the box into the backseat and climbed up front with Carly. The windshield wipers screeched as they scraped back and forth on the glass.

"You did the right thing," Carly assured Molly, with the uninformed confidence that only a close female friend could possess, and then only in foul weather.

Ben leaned weakly against his bedroom window to watch the headlights leave the parking lot, taking Molly away into the dark and drizzly night. He wasn't too proud to call after her, but he lacked the strength to make her hear his voice.

***

Lying face down on the sofa without a clear idea of how or how long ago he'd gotten there, Ben began to weigh his options. Unfortunately, forgetting Molly altogether was not one of them. How could he get through to her? He could call her cell, but she wouldn't pick up, and if she did, she wouldn't listen. A better bet was seeing her in person, but that plan presented obvious difficulties. Molly had probably gone home with her friend, and Ben had no idea where Carly lived. Besides, they would expect him to show up there and make a scene. They would have prepared to turn him away at the door, might even contact the police if he refused to leave. Alternately, if he waited for Molly to come around and see him, Ben would end up doing just what he'd promised: waiting forever. Almost without his notice, his thoughts strayed in a different direction.

He felt that he couldn't go on living without Molly, and it occurred to him that he didn't have to. While he might not have a choice about doing without Molly, he always had the option of not living any longer. The thought of suicide, abhorrent even in this time of desperate measures, brought a shudder to Ben's every muscle. Nevertheless, he couldn't resist probing its unwholesome appeal.

As he saw it, he'd either drive or jump off the Palisades out by Devoe Park. That much was clear; the reference to his turning point with Molly would be impossible to miss. He'd leave a note somewhere she'd find it, but she'd get there too late, regretting and taking back everything as he took his last gasp, crushed under all that cold, dirty water. The thought of suffocating caused Ben to shudder again, and he dismissed the logistics of his death.

He couldn't as readily dismiss the chilling but undeniable pleasure he took in picturing Molly's misery. How she would value him then, he thought, and how she would hate herself for letting him go. She'd really eat those words about never wanting to see him again. He thought of the ongoing pain she would suffer, and the overwhelming guilt she would feel. She'd be right to think it was all her fault. With any luck, she'd tell herself she'd murdered him. Years of therapy and the support of family and friends would have no effect on that damning conclusion, and she'd console herself only by writing small pathetic letters of apology to leave at the headstone of his grave. She'd never be able to read either the name on the stone, or the dates—those declaring him dead at twenty-six, and all her fault—without weeping.

This extended vision of suffering did nothing to satisfy him. He wanted Molly to regret her actions and reevaluate him in the short run, not waste the rest of her life wondering what could have been. But the concept he'd conjured up wouldn't leave him in peace, and he began to consider it a default plan in case he could find no other way to appease his horrific sense of loss, the hole in him larger than he was.

Without any real solutions to offer, Ben needed more than anything a chance to talk things over with Molly. He knew what he would tell her. They needed a new beginning. They'd gotten off to such a promising start, then things had gone downhill and they hadn't bothered to turn them around before they went too far. They needed to start over.Ben saw it clearly and incomprehensibly; he understood what needed doing, but had no idea how to do it. The vision of Molly on the cliffs looking down into the water bobbed in his head. It wasn't raining this time, but she was crying into the river, thinking about how she'd lost him forever.

Ben got out a piece of paper and a pen. A few minutes later, with something like pride in his work, he folded up the note and wrote 'MOLLY' on the outside. Newly calm, decided and even relieved, he headed to a trusted friend's house to see about the matter of its delivery. Timing was so important.

***

"Ben! Are you okay, man?" Red-eyed, disheveled, in his boxers, Jake stumbled to the door after Ben's fourth ring. Ben considered Jake's best assets for this assignment to be the vague dependability he represented, and the fact that he knew many of Molly's friends.

"Molly dumped me." Ben looked pathetic and breakable, weighed down with grief and increasingly heavy drops of rain.

"Dude. I'm sorry. Come in and tell me what happened."

"I don't have time right now. I gotta go. Can you give Molly something for me?" Ben took out the note, hoping to get Jake's word on it before he fully woke up.

"It's three in the morning, man. Where do you need to go?"

"This, here. For Molly. I'm pretty sure she's at Carly's. But don't give it to her until eleven o'clock tomorrow morning. Can you do that?"

Jake rubbed his eyes and nodded, made a careless move to unfold the paper Ben had handed him.

"Don't read it, and don't give it to her either late or early. It's a matter of life and death." Ben turned to go, regretting his melodramatic parting line.

"What is this?" Jake called as Ben slipped down the steps of his townhouse.

"Just do this for me, please. I'll call you later." Ben's reference to the future reassured his friend, as he'd known it would. While he had no intention of calling Jake, he needed time to get ready, and he needed Jake to deliver Molly's message on time. Ben stopped in the all-night district to pick up a few things before heading back to his newly empty home. He spent some time putting things together in the kitchen, thinking back to the good old days, and especially one specific good old day. From dawn until half past nine he slept, waking to worry that he'd missed his moment. He dressed, picked up the picnic basket he'd packed everything into the night before, and got into his car. It was a twenty-three minute drive to the Palisades on a good day.

The day was apparently a bad one; it took Ben more than half an hour to reach his destination. But he had no worries about the time, which wasn't yet eleven. Jake might deliver his letter a few minutes early for fear of being late, but Molly would need time to process Ben's words, burst into tears, recover and drive out after him.

***

In Carly's pale and modern breakfast nook, Molly pretended to find the comics in the *Times* amusing so Carly would stop hovering over her like a worried mother hen. At least Ben hadn't called or come by the night before; that would've been unbearably messy. She knew she'd hear from him sooner or later, though. She hoped he'd had time to pull himself together enough to listen to good sense. There was nothing more to discuss: She needed to start over, without him.

The sound of Carly's artistic wrought iron doorknocker receiving a thorough beating came from the foyer. Molly leapt to her feet, knowing it could be no one but Ben. Carly moved faster.

"I'll get it, Molly. Sit down a minute."

"But it might be Ben." Might be, nothing: Molly knew Ben could never have given up on her so quickly. Something in her squirmed, discomfited at the thought. 'Clean break,' she reminded herself. She heard Carly conversing with a subdued male voice in the other room, and waited. Carly knew her well enough not to send Ben packing outright.

"Molly, there's someone here to see you."

Molly set down the newspaper she'd pretended to read and headed into the foyer, forcing herself to breathe and to walk slowly. She needed to be strong and stand her ground.

"Hi, Molly."

Molly took a deep breath and almost lost her footing at the sight of Jake. She'd built up a small adrenalin high in preparation for dealing with Ben, and now here was someone else altogether, probably not even involved.

"Jake. It's been a while." Molly was confident that he would explain his presence. She knew Jake well enough through Carly and Ben, but not for nothing would he come see her in particular, of all times at—she glanced dubiously at the Salvador Dali-inspired clock mounted outside the kitchen—eleven am Saturday morning.

"I talked to Ben last night," Josh began, and Molly realized that he couldn't have come to see her at Carly's without having known. If there had been no breakup, he would've found her in Ben's kitchen, letting steep a cup of green tea while Ben flipped shapeless flapjacks on their charred stovetop. Molly allowed herself only an instant to think of how good she'd had it, how much more Ben had deserved.

***

Ben sat on a checkered picnic cloth spread over the hood of his car, tossing pebbles into the Hudson. He had parked illegally, but that wouldn't matter for long. The pebbles had so far to fall that he lost sight of them before they reached the water. He checked his watch again, tried to believe Molly would still appear like a vision sent to save him.

***

"Did Ben send you here?" Carly asked Jake, as Molly seemed unable to speak.

"Yes. He told me to give this to Molly." Jake produced the paper.

"What is it?"

"I don't know. Ben said it was 'a matter of life and death' for me to give it to you at eleven this morning."

Molly shuddered and tore at the paper with hands she couldn't control enough to straighten it out. "And you didn't even look at it?" she demanded as Carly helped her unfold Ben's message.

"He said not to. Don't look at me like that," Jake bristled as the women stared at him in dismay. The three read the letter in perfect silence, going over it a couple of times to be sure they'd made no mistake.

"Molly," it read, in that nervous, sloppy writing they all recognized as Ben's, "Don't you see I can't go on without you, now I know what life is like with you in it? You'll find me underwater whichever way the current runs from our spot on the cliffs. You remember the place. Don't worry about saving me, just come out here and say goodbye. I swear I'll listen to you this time. It's not your fault so don't feel bad about this."

"No!" Molly lost her balance, but Jake and Carly supported her.

"Everybody stay cool and get in my car. Molly, tell me how to get there," Jake ordered, struck by a rare flash of presence of mind.

The three of them ran out to the truck he'd double-parked in front of Carly's house. Only Carly paused, grabbing her cell phone and slamming the front door behind them. As Jake peeled out of the neighborhood, Carly turned her phone on and dialed.

"I'm calling the police." She leaned into the front seat and spoke with a firm, brutal hope. "There may still be time. When I get them on the line, Molly, you're going to have to tell me or them the exact place he'll be."

Jake sped ten, then twenty miles over the limit, swerving around his fellow drivers. If the cops pulled him over, so much the better; maybe they'd take Carly off of hold and handle this emergency.

Finally they got through to someone who sounded like he had a better idea than his colleagues what the word 'urgent' meant. Carly repeated Molly's directions to the officer, who promised to send a unit out immediately.

Deputy Sheriff Steinbeck sighed and set the phone on his desktop.

"We've got a jumper in Devoe Park out by the water," he called into the intercom. "Rogers, report to the front of the building for immediate departure. Johnson, I want emergency vehicles to follow. And give the Coast Guard and the coroner a heads-up. We may have to do some trawling in the river." Steinbeck rose from his desk and headed out to meet Rogers, stopping to check that his phone was hung up. It would've been poor policy to let those hysterical young women overhear words like 'coroner' and 'trawling'. Fortunately, he heard only a dial tone, and Rogers had pulled up in one of the squad cars by the time Steinbeck stepped out of the station to meet him.

Ben slid off the hood of his car. He smoothed the blanket back into place and got the picnic basket out of his trunk. He took out a few tarnished silver candlesticks, arranged them with rough symmetry. Across the way he made out the faint outline of the old Cloisters, like a castle in the fog. He felt unimaginably distant from everyone everywhere in the world. At least it would be a little more scenic this time.

Another look at his watch gave Ben a surprisingly late time of day; Molly was taking longer than he'd expected. It could be the traffic had gotten worse or it could be she didn't care enough to come. Ben strolled to the edge of the cliffs. He gazed down at the water, trying not to become dizzy from the white depth of the long descent.

**

Jake cursed the traffic in helpless rage, then swerved into the exit lane to cut around it. Disregarding the signs forbidding him to enter, he turned his truck onto a grassy field that Molly pointed out. Sure enough, he could see Ben's car down by the water. He would never forgive himself if this turned out as badly as it looked. Jake brought his truck to a screeching halt. Ben was nowhere in sight. Down the road a small stretch, Steinbeck and Rogers sighted him and followed his example, parking and jumping out of the squad car.

"Ben?" Molly asked the apparently unpopulated vista. She ran towards the water, and Rogers raced after her, doing his portly, middle-aged best to keep up with her young and agile panic. Steinbeck followed with Jake and Carly, who gave him a brief but lucid history and the letter to Molly.

"Ben!" Molly screamed, and everyone ran towards her. They took her cry as one of despair, until they recognized it as a greeting. There, on the edge of the cliffs, stood a lean and lonely figure, familiar to Carly and Jake even from a distance. Molly's fire-red hair trailed behind her like the tail of a kite as she flew to Ben.

"Molly!" he cried without moving from the ledge. "I waited for you. I'm sorry I did this, but I needed to see you. Tell me we can try again."

The others stopped where they were.

"Thank goodness," Carly murmured. "I really wasn't sure we'd make it."

"Somebody better get him off that cliff," Jake responded. Steinbeck took the cue and began edging towards Molly and Ben, as if afraid of startling them into flight.

As Molly took in Ben's words and the banquet he'd set up on top of his car, she realized he hadn't dealt honestly with her, and anger seeped into her grateful relief.

"So you weren't serious?" Her run slowed to a walk. "You did this just to trick me into coming out here?" Ben sensed danger and sought retreat.

"I thought about jumping. I wanted to do it." Having thought about killing himself and having actually planned to, Ben knew but didn't say, were two very different things. "I would've done it, but I didn't want to upset you."

Sirens sounded as Steinbeck's emergency reinforcements arrived on the scene. The deputy sheriff thought with pride and disinterested good humor how he'd now be able to send them away. The situation had come out better than expected. Rather than scraping this nice young man off the rocks or dredging his waterlogged body out of the Hudson, he need do nothing but keep an eye on things from a polite distance while that poor little redhead gave her boyfriend a good talking-to.

"You didn't want to upset me? Damn it, Ben!" Molly, now that she had Ben safely before her again, couldn't hold back. "How could you do that to me? Don't you have any idea how it feels to—" As she spoke she rushed towards him, whether to hug him to death or give him a good shaking, neither of them knew for sure.

But like a dog afraid of being beaten, Ben cringed away from Molly as she laid her hands on him. He'd thought she'd cry with joy, not lose what little esteem she held him in. Unfortunately for everyone involved, there was no ground behind Ben for him to step onto, and nothing to break his fall for some forty stories.

Molly screamed. Jake, Carly, Steinbeck, Rogers, and three EMT workers ran to her.

"Johnson! Patch me through to the Coast Guard," Steinbeck called into his radio.

***

Eight pairs of eyes watched the water for one hopeful sign as two aquatic emergency vehicles drifted into view, their nets already out and dragging the currents. The anxious spectators couldn't make out anything from their elevation. Rogers beckoned Steinbeck to one side.

"Do you think she meant to push him?" he whispered, still panting.

"No telling for certain," Steinbeck replied, "but I'd stake on it being a slip. No, Rogers, I think this is one of those times we look the other way and call it an unfortunate accident."

Rogers nodded. He noticed Ben's three friends looking franticly between the officers, the ambulance workers, and the river, where the Coast Guard didn't seem to be turning up much more than plastic bottles and mud. Rogers craned his neck over the cliff and made an effort to look official, lest it be thought the powers that be weren't doing everything they could to help.

"Any chance he'll make it?" he asked Steinbeck.

"Not hardly. Going over this high up, and backwards? He'd have been better off jumping. I give him one shot in a million of coming up for air."

"No, Ben," Molly agreed with the vast swath of air and water below her. "It can't be, not just like that."

Carly and Jake each put an arm around Molly and turned to lead her away from the edge. Clouds were blowing in from the East and it began to look like rain.

Bob's head felt light and liquid in the heat of late afternoon, a steamy, kissing heat that blurred some edges and sharpened others. He had spent the morning past the end of the lunch hour catching up with old acquaintances, not so old that their company strained him, but just old enough that he gained extra pleasure from the time since he'd seen them last. They had met abroad on business, and had many good old American adventures across Europe, treating the region much as one large playground with an open bar. Bob's warm-heartedness, well-formed blonde curls and muscular figure—which would tend towards stockiness later, but which suited him now, at the age of twenty-seven—had stood him in good stead with the foreign ladies, or so he and his associates liked to look back on it now.

A great reader in his earlier years, Bob had enjoyed conjuring up the picture of himself as a sort of latter-day Lord Byron. Naturally, he hadn't shared this thought with his colleagues; he had no wish to become the laughing stock of their beer-and-football circle. Bob made himself out to be the least literate of the group, referring whenever possible to 'that pussy Shakespeare'. Always painfully vulnerable to the opinions of others, he hadn't indulged in the vice of poetry since his adolescent years.

Where the vestiges of romanticism clung most stubbornly, he made the greatest efforts to conceal them. He spoke crudely of the fairer sex, though in secret he longed to find them 'chaste,' 'coy,' or at least 'cruel'. He joined and even led the gang in reminiscence of a long, somewhat fictionalized series of overseas seductions. The group had made no conquests who hadn't set out to be conquered by the next acceptable males, but not one—except Bob, when he slipped up and allowed himself to overthink the situation—was troubled with the dawning of this notion. This time, the men had spent the afternoon not only recalling their grand shenanigans on the continent, but also bemoaning—less and less coherently as their lunch hours dragged in the direction of evening pick-me-ups—the fussiness and inapproachability of the other sex on the island empire of New York.

The bar they had chosen stood, or rather sagged, in the depths of Chinatown, but the prices were low and the drinks strong. To a certain elite clientele, Bob's group among them, the house offered a variety of green and enchanting beverages, distilled on the premises, with a bitter licorice flavor that brought back some of their hazier nights abroad. Bob thought with satisfaction of an afternoon well spent as he made his way back across town. He ought to put in a few hours at his desk, but that new girl—he couldn't keep track of all these new girls they kept getting in—had been informed that Mr. Smith would be in a meeting for the duration of the afternoon, so she could cover for him. A cab, well within his means, would have gotten him to his office faster, but he was enjoying continuing the recollections of the earlier part of the day. True, he reflected, the women here didn't stand comparison with those in France, Italy, or Germany...

When unsure of his opinions, Bob tried to think in terms his companions would have spoken in. Those European women, he told himself now, taking as verbal role model his crass and under-read drinking buddy Bruce, hadn't been so quick to turn their little noses up at a few good-looking high-up business types such as themselves. Why that one broad in Paris—

But on a cobble-stoned side street in Greenwich Village a vision appeared to Bob which caused him to pause in his steps and his thoughts. He stood a safe distance away and tried to collect himself, of a sudden overwhelmed.

Her perfect slim figure stretched out against the side of the old church like an extension of the dark gothic structure itself. She wore black, or at least a very dark shade of grey, from the tips of her narrow kitten heels up. He did and didn't see her right away; at first he took her for what she best resembled, some graceful mistake in the smooth granite exterior, a wistful wisp of darkness coming from the rest of the stone mass. That these were the impressions of a man who hadn't looked at a poem since fulfilling his undergraduate English requirement wasn't as surprising as Bob would've liked to pretend; his poetic inclinations escaped most easily when confronted with either intoxication or beauty, not to mention the combined forces of the two. Then the woman moved and Bob saw that he hadn't seen her at all.

She lit a long, thin cigarette, dark as she was everywhere but her pale arms and what little he could see of her face below an ink-colored bob and the dark glasses she wore. The broad black lenses hiding her face seemed more opaque than the granite she leaned on, and had a thin glint around their borders that he didn't notice until he crept closer. The frames were edged in a strip of artificial white diamonds, the only lightness in her attire. Bob felt dizzy trying to distinguish between the girl and the building, which blurred together in spite of his attempts to concentrate. His brain throbbed confusion. Did he dare approach her, this graceful smudge in the crisp charcoal sketch of the empty church? He dared not, and yet couldn't resist. His own unworthiness didn't deter him, nor even occur to him; it was enough to draw him that she was aesthetic, striking, and darkly pure. He had no thoughts on her feelings in the matter; he wouldn't have presumed. She was to be observed, admired, if possible captured in her natural habitat, but not understood in that way.

Bob wanted both to give her something and ask her for something, in neither case knowing quite what. Whether she had as yet observed him, he couldn't be sure. Though he stood out in the middle of the sidewalk, lone and motionless among the passersby, he couldn't tell for her glasses which way she was looking. His sense of melting made its last departure, and Bob was left with a desperate urgency to make some kind of contact, break into that dark world of beauty whose passageway stood illuminated before him, blowing an invitation in smoke through parted lips.

Though he'd long ceased to read for pleasure, Bob now recalled a poem he had read and reread in his high school bedroom, but later abandoned as unacceptably emotional. Of this congenial verse but one line remained to him, which now struck him with untoward force, as no amount or quality of words ever had before.

'She walks in beauty, like the night…'

Shaking off a vain, frantic urge to recall the rest of the poem, Bob coughed into his left hand, and placed the fingers of his right in the corresponding pocket of his pants, where he crossed two of them, for luck, for protection from he didn't know what.

The graceful feminine form didn't acknowledge Bob's presence until he had twice more coughed into his hand. He couldn't think straight enough to combat his excessive sensitivity, and by the time she spoke to him, his panic resembled physical nausea.

"Did you want something?" She continued to face the street, only slightly inclining her head to indicate that she meant to address Bob and not the moving world she looked out on.

"Yes, I—have you got a light?" With relief Bob grasped this simple, perfectly acceptable request as he, swooning, would've clutched any nearby hand to keep from hitting the ground.

"Sure thing." One thin arm bent, one pale hand reached into one black pocket. She produced a lighter, black as he couldn't have otherwise imagined it, and, like the frames of her glasses, encrusted with delicate white jewels, this time in the shape of a cursive letter L. She flicked it into flame, and held it, like her gaze, straight ahead, offering it generally rather than to Bob personally.

"What does the L stand for?" Bob felt further into his element now that the ice had been broken, yet still strangely ill at ease. "If you don't mind my asking?" The flame went out, but the pale fingers and the black lighter didn't move.

> 'She walks in beauty, like the night
> Of cloudless climes and starry skies...'

"Lenora," she replied without turning.
"Beautiful."
"Where's your cigarette?"
As if she couldn't see she had enchanted him too deeply for him to have gotten one out! She who had raised his thoughts to the height of poetry for the first time in years. Bob reached first into one pocket, then another, recalling to his deep and utter dismay that Bruce had bummed his last smoke after they drank to that girl they'd known in Paris.

"I'm all out actually," Bob admitted, cramped with the shame of this failure. And still she wouldn't look at him, wouldn't see his torturous fall. Her straight-ahead gaze must now be a gentle act of mercy; she sensed and pitied, in the divine and holy blackness of her soul, his complete despair.

"Have one of these, then." The black lighter returned home safely, was replaced by a slim, slate-grey cigarette case, which unfurled to reveal a dozen or so long black beauties like the one now shrunken and drawing its last breaths between Lenora's sealed lips. "What's your name?"

"Thank you so much." His gratitude arose from both her forgiveness of his failings, and the slender gift she now offered him. With a hand tensed to keep back its trembling, he took a cigarette from the box, morbidly cautious lest he should sully her pale palm. "I'm Bob Smith," he told the dark saving grace he longed to possess, as she continued, still as a statue, to proffer the open case.

"Bob Smith? What a dull name." Lenora gave a small, ringing chuckle that seemed the very echo of itself. He could have bowed down and adored her for deigning to laugh at his name, she who stood like a granite saint outside the forgotten church, still faithfully performing miracles for her grateful congregation. "Would you get out another one for me, Bob Smith? Mine's about to go out." As she spoke she dropped the unfortunate entity to the pavement, where she didn't bother to raise her delicate heel to put out its last feeble efforts at sparks.

Veins bulging in the back of his hand with the strain of love and terror, Bob obeyed. As his hand left the case she snapped it shut, and the lighter made its graceful return. Lenora held it out ahead of her, the divine flame for him to receive. Unable to control his shaking, Bob brought the two cigarettes to it, lit them, and offered one to her. She held the flame a second longer than it had taken him to perform this ritual in her honor, then slipped the lighter back into her pocket, and put out her ash-white hand, waiting for the lit cigarette. Bob understood as if through revelation that he had committed blasphemy against her, waiting for her to reach for it from his unworthy hands. It was her part to receive, never to take. It hadn't occurred to him that a woman who could inspire such fawning devotion in him could have the audacity to exist, but he didn't regret the miracle of her presence.

"Thank you." She placed the cigarette between her lips.

How shameful that he could only offer her what was already hers. Bob knew no more words with which to worship her, but feared for his will to live if she should now or ever depart from him. Emboldened by the grave perils at stake, he made bold to go one step further in his advances.

"Listen, Lenora. I think you're very nice, and very pretty, and I'd really love to take you out sometime, get to know you a little better. How would you like that?" Wrong, all wrong, Bob lamented; surely she would now laugh, not in a ringing echo, but out of sheer, scornful disgust. How had he dared? Yet how had he sunk so quickly to these servile depths of suffering? He could think of nothing he could have done differently, no way in which he could have saved himself. As if for the last time, he let himself behold her, delicate white shoulders and hands; dark hair and glasses framing her pointed white chin and thinly parted lips; the black granite form, balancing her slight weight on thin heels and the empty walls of the church. In the still, horrific panic of Bob's thoughts, the next line of inspiration revealed itself.

> 'She walks in beauty, like the night
> Of cloudless climes and starry skies;
> And all that's best of dark and bright...'

"Are you asking me on a date, Bob Smith?" There was no cruel laughter to follow; that was certain. Lenora seemed not disgusted, but deeply, thoroughly sad. A smile slid onto her lips as she took the cigarette from them, but it wasn't one of happiness.

"Well, yes, if you'd be interested at all, I mean..." His mind blurred like the dark and light forms before him, and he couldn't shape his thoughts into words.

"Why would you want to do that, if I might ask?" Lenora's words could've killed him, had they not held that same sweet mercy.

"Like I said, you're a nice girl, and very, very— Lenora, you're the most beautiful girl I've ever seen in my life. I don't know what would happen to me if I never got to see you again. Please don't be offended by my saying this."

She laughed now, a laugh as sad and sweet as the smile it chased from her lips. She took a drag from her cigarette, reminding Bob of the one slowly burning down in his hand. He followed her example, shaking more than ever in the unbearable suspense.

"Nice? And of all things, beautiful? Bob Smith, you haven't seen very much of me yet." Another drag, and she waited, inhumanly patient, for him to collect himself and respond.

"I've seen enough of you to know I've never seen anyone like you before and if you don't know you're terribly beautiful by now…" He stopped his weakening words as she broke into a still more tragic laugh, one unbearable to hear. It sounded as if she were sobbing, but to his relief no tears slipped from under her dark and glittering glasses. He couldn't have borne her tears.

She raised a hand to the glasses, ran a thin white fingertip along the artificial diamond border of first one lens, then the other.

"Beautiful," she repeated, shaking her fine black hair, and turning towards him at last. Her slender fingers closed on the arm of the glasses, and she slowly pulled them off as if to look at him more closely.

Sickening, overwhelming horror rooted Bob to the spot even as he would've given the rest of the years remaining him to be able to run at that moment. For as she took away the jeweled frames, he didn't see the sparkling, wise eyes he had imagined, perhaps blue, perhaps brown or even hazel. Rather, he saw no eyes at all. The portion of Lenora's face which she had so wisely kept hidden was fit for a sepulcher. Where he had imagined two starry orbs of divine understanding, two deep, rough sockets gouged their way into his consciousness, calloused, brown and rimmed with puffy scars that spun a blue-grey web around each horrible hole.

In his first moment of panic, Bob imagined that they bled, but this, he found after a moment of nauseated contemplation, was only the vestiges of a natural moisture, the mucousy remnant of cut-away tear ducts. He couldn't breathe or move, would sooner have faced the Angel of Death than those two empty pits of skull. Acid vomit snaked its way up his esophagus, leaking the faint aroma of wormwood into his throat. The scarring extended past where the brows should have been, and down to the gaunt tops of her cheekbones. Though the wounds didn't look recent, the mess left behind was so gory that it hurt to see it. And now, for the first time, Lenora seemed really to look at him, to take in the sickness in his expression, to probe with bare, pussing sockets and winding purple scars the recesses of his soul.

Only by leaning against the cool exterior of the neglected house of prayer could Bob remain upright. He swallowed his rising gorge, unwilling to show his reeking disgust of her, for his next revelation was that she had seen—or rather not seen, anything but seen, sensed—this same reaction on countless past occasions, and must have foreseen it in him. He could still see all that had seemed divinely-shaped beauty, only now the blight appeared to him, gruesomely outshining all the rest, the pair of hideous skull-eyes challenging him to a grim staring contest that he resolved not to break if it killed him.

And as the damp, unnatural array of colors shone forth from her mutilated face, he forced himself to quiet his shallow breathing in deference to the grim, grey-black martyr who couldn't see but knew his weak, shameful horror.

"I'd love to go out with you sometime, if you're really interested." Lenora's lovely, horrid smile, though it took place on her unblemished lips, had the same graveside manner as the rest of her face, certain as she seemed that Bob would flee at any instant. "Why don't we swap numbers?" She reached without turning from him into the pocket of her dark slacks, and produced a flat black telephone, which matched everything about her, which also bore a sparkling letter L. No longer trembling, Bob took it and dialed as she must have to, without a glance toward the screen, feeling for the buttons as he kept his eyes on her ravaged and ravishing face.

"But haven't I told you, you're the most beautiful girl I've ever seen? Let's go right now, and I'll buy you a drink. I don't know what would happen if we never—" He began to say, 'if we never saw each other again,' but caught the slip in time, careful not to blaspheme his radiant angel of darkness— "if we never met again. Come, come, a drink right now for you, Lenora, the most beautiful girl in the City." He offered her an arm and she took it, laughing now the pure ringing laugh. She replaced her broad black glasses, glittering with that thin white border of artificial diamonds. Under the cover of the slowly setting sun, Bob's arm trembled as he led away the pale, dark figure he scarcely dared touch, looking for somewhere nice enough to do homage to her, the shining salvation of the poetry in his soul:

> 'She walks in beauty, like the night
> Of cloudless climes and starry skies;
> And all that's best of dark and bright
> Meet in her aspect and her eyes'

Bob's mind drank and drowned in perfect words. Terrified and exalted, he recalled that there were still more verses to come.

The two young women sitting across from each other at Fung Mah Palace varied sharply in degree of style and attractiveness. Laura, eagerly digging into a plate of lo mein, wore the sloppy cardigan and slacks of the undersecretary, which, on her childlike figure, gave the impression of a little girl playing grown-up. This effect was not diminished by the makeup she wore, lipstick of a cheap, blaring pink that clashed with her overgrown red pixie cut. Across from her, Carolyn, delicate, blonde, and faultless to a fault, wore a tasteful tailored suit as crisp and pale as empty eggshells, with an air to match. Her attitude stated that she knew she could do better than her surroundings, but wouldn't make a fuss. Not too much of one, anyway; she was too graceful for that. Carolyn's poise might have suggested some expensively outmoded finishing school, had she not worn it as naturally as the gold coiffure flowing sleekly down her back, which—justly—no one had ever accused her of artificially coloring.

Laura looked up at Carolyn with an overbalanced blend of emotions: one half latent envy, one half puerile joy in the admiration of perfection, and the extra half utter incomprehension. Carolyn's accomplishment of herself was a mystery beyond Laura's understanding, as was her ability to be disappointed with such an extensive array of gifts. Watching her now, Laura noticed that she was only idly stirring her fork through her food, not eating. And Laura had so hoped to impress Carolyn with this chic and current choice of restaurant.

"This lo mein is *too* disgusting," Carolyn complained, when Laura stopped eating and stared, demanding an explanation with a look, as their long history of familiarity allowed her to. Carolyn had taken, as was her custom, only a few bites before losing interest altogether.

"Shut *up!*" Laura gave her friend a shove that nearly knocked her from their rubberized red booth. "You're such a brat."

"What?" Carolyn asked, indignant.

"You're always ruining stuff for other people. I think the lo mein is great here, but now I don't even want to eat mine." Laura pushed her plate away almost as fiercely as she'd pushed Carolyn.

"Oh, no, no." Carolyn shook her head until her ironed-straight hair risked contact with both portions of noodles. "It must be this icky soda I'm drinking. They totally gave me regular instead of diet. Here, try a sip."

Laura declined, a pout on her small pink face.

"It put a bad taste in my mouth, that's all," Carolyn assured her. "The lo mein is really good here, actually. Mmm."

"Yeah, sure." Laura shrugged her round shoulders, emptily threatening to continue her sulk. She was still hungry. Her next few bites were accompanied by a frown and a pointed look at Carolyn, but then she went on more naturally. She felt guilty for eating so much when Carolyn clearly didn't like her food, but then Carolyn never liked anything. Maybe that was why she was so thin, Laura reflected. While Laura's tiny frame got her carded for R-rated movies at the age of twenty-three, Carolyn's tall and slender form more resembled the proportions of a delicate doll than those of a child. Add to that a certain shimmering air of Carolyn's that always left Laura looking dull and colorless, and there was potential for real resentment between the two.

But Laura understood Carolyn beyond her physical glamour, and wasn't fooled by her knack for assembling ensembles or the smooth purr of her voice addressing the opposite sex. In exchange for her own perfection, Carolyn paid the hefty price of incessant dissatisfaction. As long as Laura had known her, she'd taken pleasure in almost nothing but the act of being displeased, which she took little trouble to hide. In fact, it constituted the greater half of Carolyn's social contribution at any given affair. This restaurant had the rudest staff, and that one the worst sangria she'd ever tasted, half ginger ale, could she believe it? Had Laura even *seen* how low-cut that girl's top was last night, or how artificial her tan? Gosh, could she get more Long Island? Did Laura see that new movie yet? The ending was *such* a cliché. And so on, day in and day out, evening to evening, Carolyn passed her time in elegant suffering, tortured by a world that disappointed her at every turn.

Pity for Carolyn's unhappy state kept Laura from outright jealousy; she knew Carolyn's apparent sense of entitlement hid a profound fearfulness, a mistrust towards life that Laura couldn't covet. She sympathized with her friend from the distance of relative contentment. There was something endearing in the polished consistence of Carolyn's complaints.

"Oh, my gosh, I am *so* full."

Carolyn pushed aside her still highly piled plate of food, over which she'd done a poor imitation of enjoyment until Laura finished hers. "Not that it's fattening or anything," she added, in just the tone to make Laura fear that it was.

"Could the service be more slow?" Carolyn waved a third time at the hassled waitress, who all but ran over to give them their bill.

Without thinking about it, Laura reached for the fortune cookie their server left next to the check. Her mind was occupied with calculating tax and tip accurately enough not to give Carolyn cause for complaint. Not that Carolyn balked at spending money; it was only her constant regret that she threw it away on items of such inferior quality.

"I like how that waitress totally hates us." Carolyn ran a graceful hand through her hair as she contemplated this tragic circumstance.

"I don't think she hates us," Laura replied noncommittally. In a way, she thought, perhaps Carolyn did like it. She tried and failed to imitate the elegance of Carolyn's gesture in her own choppy hair, then popped open the wrapper on the fortune cookie. Breaking the cookie in half, she hoped for an amusing fortune. Carolyn had an apt sense of humor when the mood struck her.

"Hello, did you even see how she only gave us one fortune cookie?" Carolyn employed a tone better suited to discussions of unjust death sentences or large-scale violations of human rights. "She totally hates us."

"Oh, I'm sorry." Laura proffered the broken cookie to her friend, who wrinkled her nose in response. "I didn't even think about it. We can split it, or you can have it."

"Sweet of you, Laura, but I so cannot even afford the carbs after I just pigged out on all this. I mean, not that it's that much food. Like, you don't have to worry about what you eat or anything…"

"Shut up," Laura ordered her with a laugh she didn't mean nearly as much as the words it followed.

"I just wanted the fortune." Carolyn gave a maudlin sigh. So had Laura, but she hadn't really wanted it that much, and Carolyn was already having such a bad time tonight.

"Take it," she told Carolyn, biting into the empty half of the bland cookie, as if that had been what she wanted all along. "It's yours."

"Really?" Carolyn was already removing the narrow strip of paper. "Hmm… 'Learn Chinese: still single: mae yao jeh huan.' What a great fortune."

"The fortune's on the back," Laura corrected her, a little smug over the false basis of this one complaint.

In any case, Carolyn certainly didn't need to know how to say 'still single,' in Chinese or any language. She'd dated half the men in Manhattan, and it had been decidedly the handsomer and higher-salaried half. Now she was splitting her time between two gorgeous financiers who were—more than likely, knowing Carolyn— appallingly unaware of one another's existence. Not that Laura was jealous. What with work and everything, she might not have the time for a relationship, even if she could find a decent single guy. Though Carolyn, who made Laura's annual income about three times a year, seemed to manage it well enough. But of course the poor dear suffered terribly from all that her plush career and plusher boyfriends put her through.

"What?" Carolyn gasped with her usual exaggerated tone of horror, of which Laura felt somehow intolerant this evening. "I cannot even believe this. You've got to be kidding me." She waited for Laura to ask what she had to be kidding her about, then thrust the strip of paper in her face. "Read this."

"Okay." Even her own future isn't good enough for her, Laura thought, as she took the fortune from her friend. "Oh, weird. Wow. That is pretty strange." She tried not to react too strongly, as Carolyn, in her never-ending pursuit of new things to dislike and fret over, tended to take little nothings of this kind too seriously. '82309,' the slip read, 'Life will end. Be ready'.

"Oh, gosh, oh, my gosh," Carolyn declaimed poetically into her folded hands. "What if that's true? Eight twenty-three o-nine. That's tomorrow. Oh, gosh, Laura, I am going to die. I am going to die tomorrow. Oh…" Her dismay lacked some of its usual theatrical luster, and Laura hastened to reassure her.

"Don't be crazy, Carolyn. It doesn't say that at all. That isn't a date, it's just your lucky number. For people who play the lotto or whatever. And it doesn't mean you're going to die. It's probably some weird saying that doesn't translate from Chinese to English. Just throw it away. You can't go through life listening to fortunes and things like that anyway; it's all nonsense."

She couldn't think of any other way to dismiss the bald declaration of that statement, and in fact was a little shaken herself. Didn't someone proofread these things? What kind of company would print that? She looked at the wrapper, but it was only a blank and generic clear plastic. A strange coincidence, too, that the lucky number should turn out to be tomorrow's date. That must be one chance in what, a thousand? A million? But it was just that, chance, and she couldn't allow Carolyn to believe otherwise.

"Anyway, let's go." Laura pulled Carolyn from the booth, realizing as she closed her fingers around her friend's arm how frail she had become, how easily the bony wrist fit within her own short fingers.

"Fine." Carolyn followed her without resistance, but remained moody the rest of the night, too moody even to disparage anything much, and this Laura took as the most dangerous of signs. She worried all the more when Carolyn allowed them to sit some two hours in a dismal dive bar out of which she would've long since talked them any other night. Finally, at half past eleven, Carolyn admitted to the subject still preoccupying her mind, and rendering her, for the time, no threat to all the inferior persons, places and things in the city.

"I only have half an hour of safety left," she told Laura over a couple of poorly-mixed vodka-cranberries. "I am going to die tomorrow, and I totally had no time to get ready."

"You're drunk. That's ridiculous."

Yet it didn't sound so ridiculous, and certainly Carolyn wasn't so drunk. Though she always complained of a headache the morning after and dizziness the night of, she'd never been more than lightly inebriated in Laura's presence. Intoxication might have slowed her critical tongue.

"Is it?" Carolyn snapped. "Is it ridiculous?" She must be truly anxious, Laura knew; otherwise she wouldn't express her ill-humor so directly. "August twenty-third, this year, my life will end. That means I'm going to die, tomorrow."

"No, it doesn't. That's just silly. Besides," Laura argued weakly, lacking true conviction, "maybe it's a good fortune, really. It doesn't say you're going to die. Maybe it means your life will change for the better."

With an outlook like Carolyn's that seemed unlikely; as she saw things, probably the only way her life could change for the better would be to end, and give up altogether its pathetic attempts to please her.

"Maybe." Carolyn was not at all persuaded, but briefly willing to pretend. "Gosh, what a bad last night. I can't even taste the vodka in these, and am I crazy or did you hear me ask for lime?"

Laura took these words as a reassuring return to Carolyn's usual level of negativity, and smiled fondly in response. "Let's take out our tab," she suggested. "I'll call you tomorrow to make sure you're feeling okay."

***

True to her word, Laura called promptly in the first ten minutes of her lunch break, which usually overlapped with Carolyn's.

"Hello?" Carolyn's tone was blank, polite. It gave nothing away. Still, it lacked a certain liveliness.

"How are you doing?" Laura imagined a for-once haggard and rumpled Carolyn, fretting over some unhealthful vision of impending doom. She didn't like to admit that, so long as no real danger threatened her dearly dissatisfied friend, the thought of a

Carolyn who occasionally couldn't quite keep it together was not unpleasant.

"The office is simply brutal, today; I *so* won't be able to make it out for lunch," Carolyn whined brightly. "I don't even know why I let them treat me like this. But will you sneak out for a five o'clock with me? My treat. If that jackass doesn't call me before then and demand to take me out tonight. Honestly, I should just dump him," she went on. Laura knew she had no intention of doing so. It would only have cost her that much material for disparagement.

"Five o'clock sounds great." Laura hid well her disappointment. She could practically hear Carolyn's crisp blouse and slacks, not a bit wrinkled at the thought of death, over the line.

"By the by," Carolyn added, just as Laura thought the issue safely past, "you totally called to make sure I was alive. I know it. You wanted to make sure I didn't drop dead yet. Don't forget, I've still got practically twelve hours to do it in."

"I wasn't thinking that at all." Laura defended herself too enthusiastically for credibility. "I just wanted to make sure you weren't being silly and worrying."

"I've got to run, Laura, they're simply *killing* me today, ha-ha-ha." There was something artificial about Carolyn's closing laugh that reminded Laura to worry.

***

Having repented of her passive designs against Carolyn, Laura was pleased to spot her in the window of the lounge—one of the tonier ones in the neighborhood, and decidedly out of Laura's price range—where they were to meet. Carolyn had arrived early and wouldn't have enjoyed her wait; furthermore she'd had a long and trying day at work. While every other party might covet the window table bestowed upon Carolyn, the sun would be sure to glare into her eyes, and men on the street would, without fail, give her the absolute rudest looks. In spite of these apprehensions, Laura felt an at first unaccountable joy at the sight of those familiar French-tipped nails tapping the tabletop, then running gracefully through the silky golden hair that never would lie just as Carolyn liked it. Laura meekly explained to the overbearing hostess that her party had already been seated, then joined Carolyn. It occurred to her that she'd had some vague fear of their not meeting here, of unknown and ominous powers conspiring such that Carolyn would neither show up at five o'clock, nor for the rest of Laura's life.

Laura was relieved to find Carolyn's appearance largely as she'd pictured it over the phone; in spite of any minor or major tensions, neither a hair nor a thread curled out of line, and neither a grain of mascara nor the lightest smudge of lip-liner had escaped its meted-out boundaries. Only her color seemed a little off. As Laura greeted her friend, she noted that Carolyn was wearing a bit more blush than usual—perhaps a bit too much blush—and a redder shade of lipstick than it was her custom to apply. These oversights could only be a reaction against the other slight shift Laura thought she saw: a pale, almost bluish cast over Carolyn's skin, especially on the unmade-up portions of her face and throat.

Usually, Laura recalled, attempting to gauge how suddenly this change had taken place, Carolyn had a healthy glow, a flawless complexion which didn't really require the light cosmetics she wore. Had she been this pale the night before? The lighting might have been different, but it couldn't have been that different. Surely she would've noticed this almost ethereal drop in Carolyn's color. Laura tried to keep a carefree expression on her face, but was distracted by the effort of not staring too obviously. Carolyn was sensitive to things like that.

"What's with you today?" An irritable strain of excitement seemed to run beneath Carolyn's smooth and lighthearted voice. "You look as if you see—"

"A ghost?" Laura asked too loudly, almost drowning out her words with the force of the laugh she faked along with them. "No, not a one all day!"

"Interrupting is a terrible habit, not that friends like us have to play by those little rules. But I was going to say, you look as if you see a big pimple on my face, the way you're gaping at me. I'm not breaking out again, am I? My skin has been so unreliable since I was a teen; it's terrible how it affects one's appearance."

"No, you look... perfect," Laura assured her, still struggling to study the change in her friend without appearing to. In spite of Carolyn's groomed and polished state and the easy conversation she began—a string of curses against the idiots and sadists among whom she had to slave all day—she gave off a certain unwholesome aura; every few notes in her speech sounded arrhythmic, almost hectic, and there was a fuzziness, a blur about her usually distinct figure, as if she were not quite there. The edges of her, in Laura's worried eyes, flickered and shifted against the more real and vibrant background of the bar. She could have sworn that Carolyn's long delicate fingers shook ever so slightly as she lifted her margarita, and that she closed her lips just a little too tightly on the edge of the glass. Carolyn had never, Laura imagined, left a lipstick mark on anything in her life, yet here was a tense red smear around the salted rim.

"What was that?" She had lost Carolyn's exact words in contemplation of her tone.

"You are so out of it tonight," Carolyn said, her voice cracking all but imperceptibly on the last word. "I simply asked whether your day had been as wretched as mine."

"Oh, it was pretty average," Laura decided, not caring particularly about either the nature of her day or the sound of her words. "Actually, I'm kind of tired." This easy explanation for her distraction was no lie; every day of work was tiring. Not that she felt nearly as worn out as Carolyn looked.

"Of course, of course; it's brutal how hard you have to work to live in this city at all. And try staying up all night thinking..."

"Thinking what?" Laura urged her, in her eagerness leaning across the table and knocking over their half-finished second round. Their server, observing from across the room, began a dignified saunter towards them.

"Oh, dear." Laura retired back into her seat, ineffectually dabbing at the spill with a small cocktail napkin, but never taking her eyes from Carolyn. At the sound of the glasses hitting the table, Carolyn had sprung back as if a gun had gone off in her ear, and now she tensed her whole body in an unsuccessful effort to keep back the tremor that ran through her. The waitress arrived and condescended to towel up the spilt alcohol, then left to replace the casualties of Laura's edginess.

"Thinking you're going to die," Carolyn whispered. Her words sounded as if muffled by a thin plaster wall, but Laura heard them clearly, sure she'd already known them before Carolyn spoke. The server set down their drinks, and they gave her a subdued and distant chorus of thanks.

"Don't." Laura couldn't speak above a whisper, either. "You're fine; there's nothing to worry about." She pressed the issue with the first signs of desperation, as if making her closing argument against some dreadful power on behalf of Carolyn's right to be alright.

Carolyn raised her glass and drank it half off, shaking little crystals of salt onto the table, and allowing small drops she couldn't steadily hold in her glass to spatter its surface. The server, supervising from across the room, threw her a look of disdain.

"Do I look fine?" Carolyn's wavering but insistent voice dared Laura to lie and say she did. She drained off her margarita and Laura imitated her as swiftly as she could. "You've been staring at me all evening. You can see it, can't you? There are still nearly six hours left, and you can already see it."

"Don't say things like that," Laura pled, almost in tears. "You're being ridiculous."

In reply, Carolyn tossed a pile of money onto the table, not bothering to count it. She rose, swaying like a loose sheet of paper in a heavy breeze.

"Let's go, let's go. For heaven's sake, let's go."

By the last exhortation Laura had already stood and Carolyn was merely mumbling to herself. Their server began another slow and stately progress towards them. Carolyn took one, then a second shaky step away from the table. Laura watched in helpless, distant fascination as Carolyn folded in on herself with a third step she never quite made. The sight of Carolyn gently withering to the hard floor had a familiarity about it for Laura: She felt as if she'd seen it before, and in a way expected it, yet she couldn't move with any kind of speed. Leaning slightly toward Carolyn in her descent, Laura was unable to react, incapable of catching her before she fell.

The server, the hostess and the other staff, along with scattered customers from the neighboring booths, flocked around to take in the sight of Carolyn struck down.

"What happened?" someone asked, and this was echoed until a better phrasing was found.

"Is she okay?" another eager voice demanded.

The hostess barely concealed her ire at their having chosen her establishment to mar with this spectacle.

"You shouldn't let her drink like that," she admonished Laura.

"She isn't drunk, she isn't drunk," Laura told all of them. "Somebody call an ambulance."

Carolyn lay motionless, smitten by an unseen force. Someone made a phone call, and the sound of a siren broke up the small crowd a few or many minutes later. Laura rode along in the ambulance, unable to pay attention to the attempts of the EMT workers to restore Carolyn to consciousness.

In the mint-green, sterile waiting room outside of Urgent Care, Laura nervously twisted the short red pieces of her hair. She yanked on a few of them, trying to ground herself in the reality of the moment. There could be nothing wrong with Carolyn; Carolyn was an unassailable icon, not that frail shaking outline to be erased by a few letters and numbers on a scrap of paper she'd picked up only by chance.

Not a member of Carolyn's family, Laura wasn't permitted into the room with her. Hours passed, whose every minute drained that much more hope from her, but she couldn't bring herself to look up at the large clock above the reception desk. In Laura's fearful mind, each hour in which Carolyn didn't awake was a further sign that she never would again.

A damp-browed, green-masked doctor stepped into the waiting room. He slid the mask off his mouth with one rubber-gloved hand as Laura tried in vain to prepare herself for the inevitable bad news.

"You brought in the young woman who lost consciousness, didn't you?"

Laura nodded, sure she would soon collapse herself.

"She's going to be all right; it's mostly dehydration and low blood pressure that took her out, and a heavy dose of stress. She's got a slight concussion from her fall, but nothing serious. We'd like her to stay overnight with the intravenous, to be sure she takes in enough fluids and nutrients to get her levels back to normal. If I were you, I'd go on home now, give her a call in the morning, and in the future see if you can't get her to eat a little more, have a glass of water a few times a day. Right now, any anxiety or surprise could change her blood pressure so rapidly she'd go out again, but if she takes better care of herself, she'll be in good shape."

"Can I see her?" Laura asked, her eyes finally letting go of hot tears the tension of the situation hadn't allowed them to release.

"Of course. She's awake again, and doing very well." He showed Laura into a narrow, white-lit room before hurrying off to see to patients with less passing ailments, and to deliver less glad tidings to other denizens of the mint-green waiting room.

The life had flowed, as if through some magical transformation, back into Carolyn's face, which broke into a warm smile at the sight of Laura. Harsh fluorescent lighting notwithstanding, Carolyn glowed, a radiant picture of health against the white sheets of her hospital bed.

"Hi there." Laura wiped her eyes self-consciously. "You really gave me a scare."

"I actually thought I was going to die today, can you believe it? But of course you can—You thought so, too."

"Well, we can both stop worrying about that nonsense now. It's after midnight," Laura assured Carolyn, though the clock in the waiting room hadn't yet read eleven-thirty when she left it the moment before. "The day is over, and you survived. Now we can see how silly we were to worry."

"I think that's what did me in," Carolyn replied. "They say I haven't been eating enough of the right things, and that I should've refreshed myself with water instead of a couple of second-rate cocktails, but that stupid little fortune was on my mind since last night. I simply couldn't get myself feeling right about it. And now I doubt we'll be invited back to that wretched lounge, not that I mind. The service is the slowest in the area, and they put an inexcusable amount of salt on the margaritas."

Laura didn't stay long; she didn't want to tire her recovering friend. When she looked at the clock again on her way out, it was only five of twelve. Hopefully Carolyn would get a good night's sleep despite the cheap sterility of her hospital linens. Laura exited the elevator on the ground floor of the hospital, laughing to herself in pure nervous relief. Poor Carolyn. Laura blamed herself, too. Carolyn would never have taken interest in the déclassé phenomenon of a fortune cookie, had it not been Laura's first. And Laura had allowed herself to sink into an irrational state along with her friend, so much that she'd almost believed Carolyn wouldn't get up again after she fell.

In a warm haze of fondness for her friend and the joy that comes in the wake of an unfulfilled threat, Laura barely saw or heard the world around her, and even the blare of a siren hurrying to someone's aid sounded as if at a merry remove. This sense lasted only a few perfectly happy seconds. As Laura stepped off the darkened curb in front of the hospital, sudden contact with flashing lights, a screaming siren and some one-thousand pounds of speeding metal knocked her back to reality, then cut her off from it altogether. The wailing ambulance drowned out the sound of her small red head falling against the hard pavement, but according to the coroner, who noted her time of death as 11:59 pm, 8/23/09, the collision with the ambulance killed her before she landed.

This startling report didn't reach Carolyn until two days later, when her stabilized blood pressure rendered her fit to receive the news, but everyone at the funeral was surprised to see she looked a perfect mess.

The Heroes

Clare leaned against the counter, staring at the clock. Its numbers were red, square, and an hour behind. The frame was pink. The clock belonged to Susan, who hadn't looked at it since bustling in half an hour earlier and announcing that they really had to hurry, they were going to miss their film.

Now Susan was in the bathroom with Jason. He was helping her clean the tattoo she'd just gotten at a place Lisa knew in the Lower East Side. Clare forgot the name but the sign on the window had been some kind of devil, and she hadn't stayed to watch. Susan said she couldn't clean the tattoo by herself. Clare wondered what she did when no one else was home. She was supposed to treat it every two hours, and Jason wasn't always there. Clare looked at Lisa, to see whether Lisa was also watching the clock. She was. After a while Lisa noticed Clare watching her. She turned and smiled, her round, shining cheeks rising over her pointed chin.

Lisa had worried a lot about Clare since November. She didn't like to see Clare's face go blank, didn't like to see how the drawn skin stopped hiding the circles under her eyes when she stopped smiling. Clare's brown hair looked dark and heavy. She always wore it down, now.

Clare looked at Lisa a minute longer without saying anything; she knew that would make Lisa nervous, but she didn't want to say still another time that they were going to be late. She knew Lisa knew. Instead, she watched Lisa, waited for her to speak. Lisa toyed with the split ends of her unnaturally black hair, home-dyed. She should cut it again soon, Clare thought. It was getting past her shoulders, and Lisa's brown roots were starting to show, frizzy like the rest of her hair. Funny how Lisa's hair always looked so dry, but her skin always had that same wet sheen of oil, whether she'd washed it two minutes or two days before. Clare knew that if she waited, Lisa would say something. Lisa always had to say something when it was quiet for more than a few seconds. The silence made her nervous, and her face would get an overheated, red glow, a frantic hot energy she could burn off only with words.

"I'm so excited for the movie," Lisa chirped, stretching her face into forced dimples with each word. "Aren't you?"

Clare took note: That is what she thinks a smile looks like. She imitated the motions of Lisa's face, but her tight skin never formed dimples. Lisa's always dimpled more on the left cheek than the right, Clare had noticed. Susan, out of sight in the bathroom, had the thinnest face of them all, but she managed a dimple when it suited her. Clare knew this because she had noticed it before. Right now, she couldn't picture Susan's face to herself, could only picture one feature of Susan's at a time: ginger hair, pale skin, tall and thin, thin, thin. It was always that way when she tried to see people in her mind. They weren't there unless they were in front of her.

"Yes, it looks good," Clare agreed. What a waste of words. She knew Lisa thought so too. Lisa's nervous energy rose to a boiling point when she had to wait for something. Lisa was always busy, always in a hurry. She said she didn't want to waste her life. She never put on makeup, never went to a salon, rarely cleaned her room, and only showered every other day. The leftover time she spent writing, planning. Lisa wanted to be a screenwriter. She was a year younger than the rest of them but was graduating early so she could get on with her life. This was the last semester of college, for all of them but Clare. It would've been hers, too, if she were in school this semester. But Clare wasn't supposed to think about that, wasn't supposed to get impatient. Lisa was always saying she could feel herself dying every second she wasted. How she could say that, and then tell Clare to relax, was beyond Clare.

Lisa pushed herself twenty-four hours a day, three-hundred and sixty-five days a year, but she'd said, over and over again, that it was important for Clare to take her time, to do what was good for her right now. In the long run, it was more important for Clare to get healthy, not put too much pressure on herself. Lisa talked a lot about Clare getting healthy, but she never told Clare she was sick. She was painfully tactful.

"What time is it?" Lisa asked. She wanted to tell Clare she was sorry they would be late. She wanted to tell her she was sorry they were always late ever since Susan moved in, and she wished they could go back to before. Lisa wished she could tell Clare how much she missed when it had been Clare-and-Lisa-and-Jason, a team, instead of Susan-and-Jason, a couple who live with Clare and Lisa.

"Quarter of," Clare told her.

"There'll be previews." Lisa twirled a stiff, fine lock of black hair, thought of cutting it all off again. It had taken so long to grow it out this time; she'd regret it. Still, the coarse dark hair didn't feel like a part of her, and she thought of how, if she cut it off and looked at it, piled on a table or tucked into some baggie, she wouldn't recognize it as her own. How did Clare keep her hair so smooth? Even in the hospital it had looked sleek and flowing. Lisa remembered worrying that Clare would come between her and Jason, before finding out Clare was already seeing someone. How silly that worry had been.

"Are you almost ready?" Lisa called to the bathroom. "We're going to be late."

There was a blurred murmur of two voices. They weren't talking to Lisa yet. Lisa tapped her scuffed black boot on the floor. She looked at the red, square numbers on the clock. She shouldn't have told Susan it was an hour fast. Then maybe they could've gotten somewhere on time. Lisa didn't want to go to a later showing if they missed this one. She didn't want to be out late. She wanted to get up early and write. She didn't want to waste the day sleeping in.

Lisa knew Clare would agree with her. Clare always went to bed early, now. Once she'd stayed out almost every night, but now she went to bed even earlier than Lisa. Clare showered twice a day, before and after she slept. She left water on the floor each time, but Lisa didn't mind. Lisa mostly showered in the afternoon. The water on the floor, the bloated blue bathmat, let her know Clare was doing okay, was waking up and going to sleep, was home and in her room.

After Lisa got dressed in the morning, she and Clare would go out to breakfast together. When it was sunny they'd go a few blocks further east, get a sidewalk table at one of their favorite cafes in Alphabet City, looking out on Tompkins Square. On the way they saw early risers coming in and out of overgrown community gardens, the occasional suited businessperson passing by, looking a little lost this deep in the Village. Dog-walkers and shambling bums, little boys and girls in plaid Catholic-school uniforms, but mostly empty sidewalk, the freshness and privacy of early morning and the nearness of open water, visible glinting white at certain intersections on their route. Tompkins Square was a blur of green in the spring, interrupted by vague motions—the dog run, someone pushing his belongings along in a shopping cart. Clare and Lisa spoke little and enjoyed each other's company for its comfortable silence, the freedom to dream slowly into wakefulness.

They didn't eat in the apartment, because Jason and Susan were still sleeping in what had been the living room, irregularly shaped and cluttered, bounded on one end by the counter they used as a kitchen table, and on two more by the doors to Clare's and Lisa's bedrooms. Lisa always knocked too quietly on Clare's door, because she didn't want to wake them. Sometimes Lisa would slide a note under the door, and then she and Clare would tiptoe out of the apartment. The door screamed no matter how they opened or closed it, and they could hear Jason turning over in his sleep, then Susan in hers. Once they were on the stairs going down to the lobby, it was okay for them to speak again, okay to make noise.

Lisa was happy to have someone else in the apartment again, someone to wake up with now that Jason always slept in. She didn't want to get happiness out of a bad thing, didn't want to be happy the doctors had told Clare she had to be very careful, or she'd end up back in the ward. But Lisa was glad she didn't have to tiptoe out alone in the morning.

"Be right out," Susan called from the bathroom. "Just have to care for the tat." More laughter and murmurs of endearment for Jason's ears only, but which the two girls in the living room couldn't help but hear. The wall between the living room and the bathroom was very thin. All the walls were very thin.

Lisa could hear Jason laughing. She thought of how he tilted his head back before he laughed, so that the skin got tight over his Adam's apple. Of the dark stubble that cropped up on the underside of his chin no matter how often he shaved, of the rasp of his cheek against hers. Then she stopped herself. He was with Susan now. Jason was with Susan, and everything else was in the past. Jason was with Susan and not with Lisa, and Lisa wasn't angry because she'd said it was okay, she didn't mind if Jason and Susan were together. Never mind that she'd expected Susan to understand that it wasn't really okay. Lisa didn't have a right to be mad; she and Jason had never technically been together. He'd been fair game, and if it weren't for her, Susan would never have met him in the first place.

Clare narrowed her eyes and stopped smiling once she could tell Lisa wasn't checking on her anymore. Her natural expression wasn't a smile, but Lisa worried so much. She wanted Lisa to think she was happy. She wanted everyone to think she was happy, because she didn't want to end up in the hospital again. Living with Susan was a blessing compared to living there. Clare wondered how her face had looked before they put her away, whether it had looked like Lisa's did now. Lisa's wide green eyes were stretched and shining, but she wasn't looking at anything in the room. Her skin looked slack and greasy, now that she wasn't shaping it into a smile. She's thinking about Jason, Clare thought; she's thinking about Jason the way I used to think about Mark.

Lisa was trying very hard not to think about Jason. Susan was her friend, and they all had to live together: It wasn't good for her to think about Jason anymore.

Clare watched Lisa catch herself, watched her flinch and stretch the smile back onto her face, look back at Clare.

"It never took me this long to take care of mine," Lisa told Clare. Lisa had gotten four tattoos in the three years since her eighteenth birthday and never made a fuss. But now that Susan had her first one, Clare noticed Lisa had started talking an awful lot about her four tattoos, about the fifth one she was planning on getting. Jason had two tattoos, but talked about them as if he were an expert. Clare didn't have any. She was afraid of commitment and tired of needles.

Lisa thought of Jason holding Susan's hand while the needle buzzed over her the night before. Had he held it the same way he'd held Lisa's a year before, or was it different because he and Susan slept in the same bed? Lisa wondered whether Jason would hold her hand again if she went and got a new tattoo. She wondered if he'd rub ointment on hers the way he did on Susan's now. He hadn't the last time, but she hadn't asked him to. She would've been embarrassed to be so forward. But Susan wasn't embarrassed.

"Do you want a cup of cocoa, while we're waiting?" Clare asked. She wanted something for them to talk about, something for them to do.

"Oh, I'll get it." Lisa jumped up. She'd been that way ever since Clare had been allowed to come back: motherly, smothering. She didn't let Clare do anything for herself anymore, always seemed to worry that Clare would somehow get hurt.

"No, never mind," Clare told Lisa before she could get her hands on the grease-spattered pot resting on their rusted gas stove. "Let's just go down and get some." Clare felt as overheated as Lisa looked, but she burned with sluggish panic, not frenzy. She needed to get out of this apartment, into the air, to feel the rush of traffic speeding down the broad avenue, to orient herself along the order of a neat grid of streets. She didn't want Lisa to boil water and fill the apartment with steam. She didn't want to wait for Susan any longer.

"Okay, great," Lisa agreed, too cheerful. That was how she always sounded when Clare asked for something. Too cheerful, too quick to agree.

Lisa couldn't decide whether they should leave without Susan and Jason. If they left right now, they could make the movie, and stop for a cup of hot chocolate on the way. They'd get to the theater in plenty of time, but she hoped their showing wouldn't be sold out. She should've gone by and gotten tickets earlier, but she hadn't expected them to leave so late. She should take Clare and go now, say that they were getting hot chocolate, getting tickets, saving seats, anything. She didn't like when Clare got that panicked look on her face; it made Lisa feel as if something terrible were about to happen, and only Clare could see it coming.

Before Clare could respond, the bathroom door opened. Lisa watched thin, pale-orange Susan, elegant in her short, short white dress next to too-tall muscular Jason, with his black hair and his heavy five o'clock shadow, the tattoos on his arms and the ring through his eyebrow. They don't go well together, she thought, looking at Jason's dark, rumpled clothes. Though Lisa had dyed both the same day, Jason's hair hadn't faded the way hers had, and the color looked better on him. She knew Susan didn't like Jason's hair black; she thought it was punky and immature. Lisa had quickly, too quickly agreed to dye Jason's hair along with her own. It was her way of marking him, claiming him as still hers. She wanted people to see them and think they went together.

Clare watched Lisa staring at Jason and felt embarrassed for her. Couldn't she see she was making both him and Susan uncomfortable?

"Let's go," Clare said. "We're going to be late."

"Yeah, fine." Susan languidly pulled away from Jason's side to pick up her purse from the countertop, where she'd left it beside the clock. She felt a twinge of guilt under Lisa's long hungry stare, the sudden turning away of her eyes. But that was unfair. Susan had nothing to feel guilty about. Was it a crime for her to try and be happy, just because Lisa couldn't be happy herself?

Lisa continued to look away. She didn't want to see the time, didn't want to see Susan's casual comfort in her home.

"Let's go," Clare repeated as she and Lisa stepped out the door.

Susan didn't answer this time. Clare had been getting on her nerves for a while now. At first she'd felt bad admitting this, because Clare had been so sick, in so much danger, and Lisa and Jason had been so afraid for her. But now Clare had been on outpatient leave for a month, and Susan was tired of playing nurse. Clare seemed fine most of the time, and if she wasn't fine, they shouldn't have let her out. Why did Lisa keep babying her? Just because Clare had wigged out didn't mean she got to have her way about everything. Susan took an extra long time coming out of the apartment, but then noticed that Lisa, unlike Clare, hadn't trotted downstairs, was still waiting outside their door. Susan smiled but didn't look straight at her. She knew Lisa wouldn't notice. Lisa was always looking at Jason.

That annoyed her, too. It's okay, Lisa had told her before; there's nothing like that between us. I just want you two to be happy. Bullshit. Whatever Lisa might tell herself, she wasn't doing anybody any favors with her drab, tiresome personal martyrdom. Not Jason, who preferred lighthearted, upbeat people, and certainly not Susan, who too often found herself cast as the lion to Lisa's Christian-in-the-Coliseum persona. Not even Clare, the ostensible reason for all of this, for the way Lisa had become. Susan pulled Jason's arm around her. She stood up extra straight with her shoulders back so that the design on her chest would show over the top of her dress.

Lisa looked at the inky maze of roses, glistening with ointment. She couldn't help but picture Jason rubbing it on for Susan. Sick to her stomach and embarrassed that Susan had seen her looking, she ran downstairs after Clare.

Out on the avenue, Clare and Lisa soon stepped around the dawdling couple, took the lead. The sky had drifted from daylight into New York's perpetual twilight, its unsatisfying surrogate for night. Streetlights and corner delis, thousands upon thousands of residences and businesses lighting up the darkness, forming together an artificial sun that knows no setting, and by which no one can guess the hour of the night.

Clare didn't think getting to the movie on time concerned Susan and Jason; they'd just make out the whole time, anyway, and grab each other whether or not it got scary. She'd better sit next to them and let Lisa be on the end. It would hurt Lisa to be close to them.

Clare wasn't talking, had that same vague look in her eyes. Street after street they crossed, regardless of the pedestrian signals, of the white go-ahead sign or the flashing red hand cautioning them to stop. Lisa made sure to watch where they were walking so Clare wouldn't wander into traffic with that unseeing stare. The lovers behind them were just as liable to step in front of a car. Lisa thought she'd better suffer through sitting next to them in the theater rather than forcing Clare to. Clare hadn't been interested in anyone since Mark, and that made sense, but Lisa didn't think she liked to be around couples anymore. And Lisa didn't want Clare to think of anything sad.

Even so, Lisa dreaded sitting next to Susan and Jason. They always had to make such a spectacle of themselves. If she and Jason were together, they wouldn't make the other people in the theater uncomfortable. Jason used to be happy just watching movies. Lisa thought of all the old movies she and Jason had watched together. Whenever Clare had been out with Mark and it'd been just the two of them in the apartment, they'd piled up the blankets and watched one on the sofa in the living room. Lang, Murnau, Freund—the classics. That was before they moved the sofa out to put in a bigger bed, a bed big enough to fit Susan and Jason together. Before they'd pulled a curtain across that part of the apartment and screened Lisa out of Jason's life.

Lisa caught herself thinking of that too much, but as long as she kept looking straight ahead, no one could tell where her thoughts were. She thought again of Jason sitting next to her on the sofa, the sinking cushions letting their weight slide towards the center. They'd sat arm to arm, skin touching and so close, and it hadn't meant anything. And then it had.

Lisa looked over at Clare. Clare wasn't looking at anything. But Clare had always been thoughtful. She'd looked that way a lot, even when she first moved in with Jason and Lisa, when she was still with Mark. Lisa remembered how Clare had looked at Mark, the way her face had come alive then, all her happiness taken out of storage for the occasion. They'd all been such good friends; Mark was over almost as much as the three of them, and when he wasn't, Clare was with him. And then Jason and Lisa had seen Mark put that look on another girl's face, had seen him where he shouldn't be. Lisa had thought it was her job to tell Clare. Mark was her friend, but Clare was her friend first, and Mark was in the wrong.

Lisa still thought she'd done the right thing. That's what Jason had said, even when he'd had to come into Lisa's bedroom and close the door while Clare and Mark screamed at each other, and Jason and Lisa pretended not to hear. He'd said it again while Clare was puking in the bathroom later, after Mark had left for good. Don't worry, he'd told Lisa over the sound of coughing and heaving, you did the right thing. If it was the right thing, Lisa always wanted to ask him, why didn't you do it yourself?

Clare had put herself away after that. She wouldn't come out with Jason and Lisa, wouldn't eat, wouldn't get out of bed. That was okay, because Clare was supposed to be upset. You were supposed to be upset when you found out your boyfriend had been cheating for months. But not forever. After a few weeks, Jason and Lisa had had a meeting about Clare. They were worried. Clare hadn't answered the calls from her work until she didn't have work anymore.She was going to fail the semester, if she didn't get out of bed.

Lisa looked at Clare now and said a small prayer for her to be okay. She'd gotten so fragile last fall. Clare was looking down at the sidewalk, and Lisa wondered what she was thinking. Was she watching the chips of quartz glisten under the pale street lights, or counting irregular black circles of tar and chewed gum? Was she remembering, or was she living, this moment, right now?

Clare noticed Lisa looking at her and smiled until it hurt. She looked back at Jason and Susan, then tried to exchange a glance with Lisa, roll her eyes at how slowly those two were walking. But Lisa wasn't paying attention. Clare wondered what she was thinking. She hoped Lisa wasn't thinking of Jason.

You have to get out of bed, Jason had told Clare after three weeks. Three weeks of her spitting out what Lisa fed her and barely making it to the bathroom. Three weeks and only a handful of words, most of them curses, some of them unintelligible. Jason and Lisa had decided it would be better if Jason said something. Clare and Lisa might have gotten into a fight about it, because they were closer, but if Jason said something, Clare would have to listen. She and Jason got along, but she'd only known him since she moved in. Okay, Clare had said. Lisa remembered listening from the sofa in the living room, waiting for her to say more. But that was all. Clare had said okay. You have to take care of yourself, Jason had said. We're here for you.

And Clare had gotten out of bed. Had gotten out for as long as she'd been in it, and then it got worse. The few times Jason and Lisa saw her that fall, she'd been barely the bones to hold her skin in the shape of a person. She'd grown black rings above her eyes as well as below them, and covered herself with small scabs that never seemed to heal. Nothing she'd said made sense, until she came home that last time, and lay down in her bed. I'm tired, she'd said. They didn't know where she'd been the past week and were afraid to ask. Clare got mad when they asked.

Lisa and Jason hadn't known what to do during all those weeks. Lisa especially felt she should be looking out for Clare, but Clare got so angry when she tried to check on her, and then she became cruel. Stop bothering me, she'd slur if Lisa called to ask when she was coming home. You're pathetic. You think you can tell me what to do, but you're fucking pathetic. She'd said a lot of other things, but Lisa hadn't told Jason about those. She'd tried not to hear them, either. Clare's just upset, she'd told herself. She doesn't mean those things.

That last time Clare had come home before she'd gone away, she'd smelled even worse than she'd looked, which was like death. Lisa could tell she'd vomited on herself, and Clare had blood all around her lips, on the insides of her nostrils, drying in little brown flakes. Her eyes had been yellow, like a sick dog's. I'm tired, she'd said. Lisa and Jason called Clare's mother a few times, but no one picked up. Lisa had wiped off Clare's mouth and forced her to eat and drink while Jason propped her up. Later Lisa helped Clare into the bath while Jason waited outside. She'd looked away from Clare's thin, scabby body, ashamed of her own disgust, her secret wish to pass this problem onto anyone else. I'll get you a towel, she'd said, because it was all she could think to say, because it was a reason to leave.

She and Jason had sat on the sofa while Clare lay in the bathtub. Lisa wanted to ask Jason whether he thought Clare would be okay again, but she knew Clare could hear from the bathroom, so she said nothing. I'll check on her, she'd said after a while, and then she'd knocked, come in when Clare didn't answer. Clare's head hung lazily over the rim of the tub, one arm reaching for the dusty tiled floor, the other making the bath a soiled soupy pink. She'd only gotten through one wrist before she quit. That was the first thing that occurred to Lisa, that Clare hadn't even made it that far.

The ends of Clare's hair were getting wet on one side, but she was slowly breathing more small rust-colored flakes out of her nose. It wasn't even a surprise. Lisa's only surprise was how calmly she called the ambulance, how much she seemed to have known this would happen. Jason had put his arm around her shoulders while they rode in the ambulance with Clare. Lisa wanted him to carry her away to anywhere else.

"I could totally go for a white chai latte, anyone?" Susan interrupted the silent thoughts of the small walking party. They stopped at the corner to consider her suggestion.

"Clare wanted some hot chocolate," Lisa told her.

Susan rolled her eyes at Jason, willing him to understand her annoyance. So what if Clare wanted hot chocolate? When was it going to be important what she, what anybody but Clare wanted? It wasn't like Clare was going to slit her wrists over whether they got chai or cocoa.

Jason looked from one girl to the next, but didn't return Susan's look of frustration. He didn't want to think of his girlfriend as selfish, but the way she was about Clare embarrassed him. It seemed like every time they were alone together, Susan had a new complaint about Clare, or about Lisa's taking care of Clare. Jason was tired of hearing about it. It made her sound bratty and inconsiderate to complain that Lisa coddled her sick friend, that Clare got her way too often. Jason wished Susan could be more like Lisa, who never put herself first. Lisa, who'd told him it was the wrong time for them to be together, they needed to look after Clare. Poor unsuspecting Lisa, who'd brought Susan into their home and not thought anything would change.

A lot of people would've thought Jason went for Susan over Lisa because Susan was prettier, thinner, more glamorous. Because

Susan was confident and cool, and good in bed. But that wasn't it, exactly. Jason thought Lisa was pretty too, maybe in a more original way than Susan. Lisa had big bright green eyes, almost like a cat's. Jason had never seen anyone with eyes like that. She had a nice enough figure under her baggy, mismatched clothes, and when she smiled you couldn't say no to her. She was sweet, which Susan was anything but. Given the choice, Jason might've gone for Lisa, almost in spite of himself. But Lisa hadn't been available to him, not that way. And then Susan had been there and interested and very, very available. Jason had thought there might be something between him and Lisa earlier, but she'd never let on that they could be together after that one night, never been anything but friendly, and Jason figured she wasn't interested, was just avoiding hurting his feelings.

But other times he'd catch her looking at him with those wide, nocturnal-looking eyes, and wonder whether she hadn't wanted more from him, after all. If so, she'd gotten less than she started out with. He and Lisa never talked anymore, never did anything anymore. Susan was always there, and if coincidence left him alone with Lisa, Lisa always had some place to be. He missed her.

"Didn't you want some hot chocolate, Clare?" Lisa asked, dimpling the left side of her face.

"Yeah, sure," Clare muttered. She wasn't a child. She could get something herself if she wanted it. She didn't need Lisa to speak for her. She was almost angry, but then she saw the sad desperate smile lighting up Lisa's face, and remembered that Lisa was on her side, Lisa only meant well. She thought of all the times Lisa had come to visit her in the hospital, the way Lisa had pretended everything was normal and they were just hanging out. She'd brought an artificial cheer that must've been exhausting to produce. The vestiges of it were still there, but Lisa had worn it thin trying to cover the past few months.

"Shouldn't we stop here, then?" Susan was already stepping in the direction of the small boutique, across the avenue and over one block, where she could satisfy her craving in a guiltless, under one-hundred calories fashion, and take it to go in a designer-logoed trademark recycled paper-plastic blend carry-cup. Because she cared about the environment and staying healthy and things like that. She wasn't watching her weight, just keeping an eye out for it. Which was more than she could say for the rest of them. Lisa was on the lighter end of the spectrum, but since she dressed like the maternity department of the Salvation Army, who could tell what she weighed? Clare had put on at least ten pounds since moving back in, maybe thanks to the homemade cookies Lisa kept foisting on her like they were the latest FDA-approved antidepressant. Lucky for her she had the room to gain the weight. Another victory for the schizoid diet and fitness program. Actually, Susan didn't know exactly what was wrong with Clare. Lisa acted like the whole thing was CIA-certified confidential. It was practically illegal to use the word 'sad' in the apartment.

"Hold on," Lisa called after Susan. "Clare thinks we should go somewhere closer to the theater. And I do, too," she added, as if this were hardly worth the mention.

Jason didn't want to get involved. He felt that, as usual, the girls were really arguing about something else, but he couldn't give a shit whether they drank tea or whatever the hell it was now. He turned away from the group, pretended to examine the window display in the high-end children's store they'd paused in front of. The lights were turned out for the day and a metal grate pulled down over the glass. The porcelain dolls behind the bars had a guilty, frozen look, little inmates on death row, hoping against hope for a rescue. He looked over at the girls, not knowing what thought they were lost in, and found they would've fit a little too perfectly in that unlit window.

"Well?" Susan asked him. Jason looked up and realized he'd been staring at Lisa, and a pale flush of blood had come into her face. She looked at him—a timid, scattered glance whose brightness faded like the taillights of taxi after taxi speeding downtown—then pretended to be interested in what Clare might say.

"Maybe we should walk towards the theater in case it's selling out," Jason said. With the thought that there might be no more tickets, he had an uncanny certainty that they wouldn't see the movie tonight, and the walk to the theater seemed long and full of dread. But the other three tended not to disagree with him, and the parade continued towards the cinema.

As they neared SoHo, the sidewalks were more than ever full of people, mostly young, all dressed up for a night out. Some were drunk and some were in love, and many huddled laughing on street corners, forcing the four moviegoers to weave around them in a fragile chain, Clare at one end and Susan at the other. Downtown Saturday night, this festival air, had never seemed so alien to Jason. He had the feeling that this was some morbid, last-ditch celebration, a merrymaking on the eve of the apocalypse. He wanted to go somewhere quiet, even if only for a minute. He wanted to step back and look around him, to know where he stood.

A few blocks from the theater they approached a favorite café of Clare's and Lisa's, the one Lisa had taken Clare to when she first got out. They'd sat at the window table and talked, or Lisa had talked. Lisa had said a lot of happy things very, very quickly. Clare had mostly watched her, tried to imitate the look on her face. She was still on a lot of medication, and could only slowly form responses. Clare saw Lisa give a small look to the place. She wouldn't ask to go for herself.

"Why don't we stop here and get drinks?" Clare suggested.

"That's a good idea," Lisa agreed. She'd been thinking they should stop there. She knew it was Clare's favorite, and they also had chai, so maybe Susan wouldn't complain too much.

"Yeah, it's a bit chilly for April," Jason agreed. "I could go for something to warm me up." He turned into the café before Susan could either offer her services in that department, or try to take them somewhere else. They had to step around a small mewing grey cat to get in; it tangled itself around their legs and didn't seem to belong anywhere.

"Aw, wook at the wittle bitty kitty," Susan cooed in the same voice she used to address Jason when someone else was listening.

"A medium soy hot chocolate," Clare told the man behind the counter, who seemed annoyed to have to take a break from leering at Susan. There was a bowl of fruit next to the cash register, wilting oranges and browning bananas. Clare couldn't believe anyone would buy any of it, and wondered what sick thing was hiding beneath those softly rotting forms, poisoning them with its foulness. She forced her eyes to the screen next to the cash register, telling her how much money she needed.

"The same," Lisa added, before the man behind the counter could start making the first one, "please." She and Clare tended to order the same thing, but Lisa always let Clare go first. It was as if she didn't think her own order important enough to trouble anyone with, except as an addendum to Clare's.

"Make that three," Jason spoke up. He turned to Susan.

"I don't want anything," she snapped, as if her conversation with the cat had used up all the gentleness she was capable of.

"Are you sure?" Lisa asked, desperate to keep everyone happy. "They have really good chai lattes here."

Susan didn't respond. Jason treated the group and they stood at the corner waiting for their drinks. Susan decided she preferred the cat to all of them, and sat down at the bench in the window, stroking it idly. Let them hurry. She couldn't care less whether they made the movie. Why did Jason insist on these little group outings? Yeah, we're all supposed to be friends. She got it. What she didn't get was what Jason wanted with that pair of sad-sacks. If he'd wanted Lisa, he'd had time enough for that before she moved in. Lisa. The little saint of Third Avenue with a heart that bleeds for everyone. But her kindness was cheap—Susan couldn't value something so bountiful, so readily available. Lisa had told Susan she could stay—just for a month or so—because she and Jason couldn't make the rent alone, and she didn't want Clare to have to worry about that, on top of everything else. The little grey cat twined around Susan's left ankle, and she stroked it behind the ears.

On top of everything else. That was Lisa's catchphrase when it came to Clare. I don't want Clare to stress about that, she'd say, on top of everything else. On top of what else, exactly, Susan wanted to know. Clare had taken the semester off, wasn't looking for a job. What she did all day other than complain, stare into space, and send Lisa on errands was a mystery to Susan. No, it couldn't be Clare who interested Jason, unless in a charitable kind of way. And Jason wasn't the love-thy-neighbor type, except where Lisa came into the picture. Was he doing this for her? Getting them together as an excuse to spend time with Lisa?

Susan looked over at the three of them, juggling lids and napkins, spilling and wiping up. Lisa had that usual dumb, timid look on her face, and that's all she had. But Lisa's very inferiority threatened Susan—Jason must see something she couldn't, meaning she was missing—what?

The mewing grey cat wound itself tighter around Susan's leg. She looked to see whether anyone was watching, intending to kick it away before it could leave too much of its scent or hair behind. But then she held back. It didn't seem stray—it was too clean, too used to people—and it was a clever little beast. Wasn't rubbing up against holier-than-thou Lisa, was it? The animal had taste, you could see that. Let the rest of them treat her like a wicked stepmother—Susan didn't see Clare or Lisa troubling themselves over this fellow creature.

"Excuse me," Susan addressed the cashier as soon as the rest of them were ready to leave. "Whose little kitty-cat is this?"

"He bothering you, Ma'am?" The greasy older man brushed one hand against the other as he looked Susan up and down, apparently ready to throttle the objectionable feline on the spot.

"Oh, no, I just wanted to make sure the wittle baby has a place to go," Susan simpered. She bent and lifted the squirming, bony mass to herself, careful to keep its fur from her tattoo. Who knew where it'd been. No use worrying about the hair on her clothes right now. Tomorrow afternoon she'd run the dress down to that little old Chinese lady at the dry cleaners.

"Yeah, poor little guy." The cashier converted into an Assisian on the spot. "I dunno where he belongs, but it sure ain't here. Boss called animal services couple hours ago. Should be here soon to pick him up."

"Wonderful," Lisa broke in, relieved to hear that someone was coming for the little stray, and that it wasn't their problem. She looked at Clare and dimpled both sides of her face. Once she and Clare would've laughed at this, the idea of someone like Susan rescuing a kitten. But not now. Clare wasn't drinking her cocoa, wasn't looking at anything. Her mouth was set, as if she were about to cry or scream. She stepped around Susan and the cat, stood by the glass door facing out. Lisa hurried to her. Clare always seemed on the point of running away.

It wasn't her physical disappearance that worried Lisa, but the blank look in Clare's eyes, the dull, unlit brown of them. Clare could go away into herself again at any moment. It had taken the doctors months to pull her out the last time, and she wasn't really all the way out yet, hadn't ever come all the way back to herself. It wasn't the drugs, the doctors had said, although those might have caused permanent damage. It wasn't the drugs and it wasn't the breakup. Those were just triggers. Something inside of Clare had been waiting to go off, something Clare had held in for a while, could hold in most of the time, and then couldn't any longer.

It wasn't until Lisa's third visit to the hospital that Clare told her she'd been there before. Not to this hospital, but in the psych ward. The last time had been two years before, a year before they'd first lived together, almost a year after she'd started seeing Mark. He'd helped her through it. Clare didn't say what she'd been there for. Lisa didn't ask and Clare didn't tell. It didn't seem to matter at the time. The only important labels were sick and well, and they both knew which was Clare's.

Lisa hadn't known what to say. When they'd brought Clare there, she'd thought, this is just a bad thing that happened to Clare. Something bad that could happen to anyone, like getting in a car accident. Then, finding out about those other times, she'd seen that the sickness had always been there, hiding behind Clare's blank looks and distracted remarks, waiting for its chance. A trigger, the doctors had said. What would be the next one?

Being with Clare had been a burden after that, sometimes lighter and sometimes heavier. The Clare Lisa had known was gone and would never come back. Had never really been there at all. Lisa's vision of her friend as strong, as whole, had been an illusion. Clare had been a glass figurine in the shape of a fortress, and Lisa had taken her for the real thing. Then Mark had dropped her on the ground and shattered her, and no one had been able to put the pieces quite right since. Clare's fragility was terrifying.

Lisa couldn't say this aloud, not to anyone. Before Susan she might've expected Jason to understand, but they didn't tell each other anything anymore. Lisa had to watch what she said to all of them now, but especially to Clare. She had to screen out words that would make Clare unhappy, would put the panicked expression on her face, the one that preceded—Lisa didn't know what, but that face always made her look over her shoulder. And there was never anything there.

Lisa could sense Claire's moods as no one else could, could tell when she was about to become upset over some false word or reminder of sadness, and gently guide her away from it. For a long time Clare had been convinced that no one could understand her, had cried when someone didn't follow one of her confused remarks. Lisa had become a translator, communicating what Clare couldn't, and making communications from others safe for her to receive. So it was Lisa's responsibility, Lisa's private burden, to take care of Clare. Because no one else could. No one else could read Clare, and now she saw a look on Clare's face she'd come to recognize, anger and fear and confusion over something only Clare could see. Lisa needed to drive it back into Clare so the good feelings and logic could come out again. Once she'd thought she could chase away Clare's fears and irrationalities, but now she knew she could only chase them back where they'd come from, inside of Clare.

"Why don't you put our little friend back down, Susan," she suggested, trying to keep her voice light, trying not to let Susan know how much depended on this for her, for Clare, for all of them, "so he can get rescued."

"Some rescue," Susan snapped, gripping the cat until it made an ungrateful yowl of complaint. "They'll take him to the pound and put him to sleep with all the other strays."

"Do you know that for a fact?" Clare still faced away from Susan, glared out the door. She almost seemed to be talking to herself. But Lisa could feel the heat of their dislike for one another passing through her, subtle yet piercing as the sun in a magnifying glass. Sweat crept up her hairline, slipped back down. She looked to Jason for the support she knew she couldn't count on him to provide.

"Yes, I know it for a fact. Come on."

Lisa couldn't tell whether she was talking to the cat or to the rest of them. Watching Susan clip out of the café switching her narrow hips, Lisa was reminded of an angry swan, the threatening shake of white tail feathers preceding an attack. The cat must belong around here, must've gotten lost from somewhere. If they took it away, how would the owners ever find it again?

But the cat wasn't her real worry. Clare was fixed on it now, but surely seeing something else. Her tight face looked on the point of bursting and her lips shaped small sounds, not quite words. An endearing nervous habit, Lisa and Jason had thought, before it became a symptom, a sign.

"What are we going to do with it?" Jason asked when they'd regrouped on the sidewalk out front. He was conscious of the patrons in the café, of the greasy cashier watching them through the glass doors. He was conscious of their small, tense circle, and Clare standing outside of it. Fixed among the passersby heading uptown, downtown, the group stood, as if they had never existed outside of this moment, this street corner, this inertia. Jason switched his cardboard cup, half drunk and no longer appealing, from hand to hand, waited. Wouldn't something turn up? He looked at Clare, who couldn't see him back right now. He looked at Lisa. Her shining eyes caught the streetlights, as they always did at night, but reflected in them now he saw his own frustration, the growing desperation of the group. Desperation. Was that what this was? Over a cat? Over nothing. He wished they'd start walking again. They'd gotten to a bad place.

He turned to Susan, tried to plead with her narrowed auburn eyes. "Babe, you can't expect us to—"

Lisa anticipated Jason's anxiety, adopted it as her own. "The lease says no pets," she told Susan, with all the firmness she was capable of. Technically the lease also said no Clare and no Susan. Lisa and Jason had signed together, but they'd known they were going to need someone else. When had they stopped needing each other?

Lisa and Jason. Even with all the official jargon in the way, Lisa had liked the look of their names together on that paper, the twelve-month lease. Connected to each other in the eyes of the law, like a little piece of marriage.

She and Jason went back a couple years now. They'd gone to all the same shows, hung around afterwards trying to make friendly with all the same bands. They'd stumbled accidentally into acquaintance, and by the third or fourth time they met, felt like lifelong friends. Lisa had loved Jason from the beginning, or maybe she only told herself that afterwards. But he never gave her any sign that they were dating, and by the time they moved in together, it seemed as if they were too close for that. Until that night, a week after Clare had gone to the hospital. But now that was gone too, all of it was gone. Lisa went to her shows alone, or sometimes with Clare. Jason's weekends were reserved for Susan. All of him was reserved for Susan.

"What about the movie." Clare appeared to be speaking to the cat in Susan's arms, a posture that would've been amusing if not meant so seriously.

"How can you—" Susan began, before Jason's hand on her shoulder stilled her indignation. "Oh, why don't you all go ahead," she purred, dangerous with the foreknowledge of her success. "I'll miss the movie. Someone has to take care of the wittle babykins." Only Susan's arms, her chest, the parts of her touching the little animal she held, felt warm, alive. She had the eerie feeling of a sleeper between dream states—knowing only that the things around him aren't real, yet unable to recall what is.

Jason and Lisa broke into aimless protest. Clare looked indifferent, maybe unaware that Susan had spoken, maybe deliberately so. Lisa would've been happy to let Susan go, but she knew Susan would take Jason with her. Take the last of him away and leave Lisa alone with what Clare had or was about to become. And it didn't make sense for her to go, wherever she was going. It didn't make sense to take so much care of just this one creature. A creature Lisa was certain they wouldn't be able to save, were only putting off giving up on.

"Susan, if you'd passed this cat on the street," Lisa began, then stopped, knowing her question would come out an accusation. If Susan had passed that cat on the street, passed a bum, passed Clare, Lisa, anyone in need of help, she wouldn't have stopped. Susan was the type to wear furs but sign petitions for animal rights. She'd drag them all over the city for this kitten, but the hundreds or thousands of other strays wouldn't cause her a moment's heartache. It wasn't hypocrisy, just a limited understanding. The way a child would look at it, Lisa thought. But Susan was no child, didn't have that soft innocence to excuse her fickleness. At the other end of the block a streetlight flared brighter than all the others, then went dark, erasing the strip of sidewalk below it.

"If you don't care about it, Lisa, that's fine. But I care." Susan urged Jason in her kitten-voice to regard her ward's sweet wittle face. He obliged, didn't seem to know where to go from there.

"If we got there in ten minutes," Clare spoke up. She didn't acknowledge the question of the cat, or of Susan.

"Go to the theater, then," Susan snapped. She felt helpless, up against some force vast and towering as the city itself, dark as those unlit squares of sidewalk. Helpless to save even one small, warm body, as if, no matter how tightly she held it, she'd soon wake to find her arms empty, her chest cold. "Go right ahead."

Clare looked ready to, ready to go off but not to the theater.

"Wait," Lisa urged her, all of them. The main problem was just to get rid of this cat. Get it off their hands, and start the night over from there. They didn't have to see a movie, didn't have to do anything. Just get back to where they'd been before this. "There's a little animal rescue around the corner on Fourth Street," she recalled. She'd recently noticed the place on her way to a coffee shop she liked to write in, and now almost believed it'd been for a reason.

But it was only a coincidence. She'd fall into the same trap as Clare if she looked for a meaning in everything. Clare had started to explain that to her in the hospital, the reasons for everything, the whole dark conspiracy going on around her. When Lisa had tried to suck the poison out of Clare's fears, to bear some of them for her, they'd been too much, and she'd come home to Jason feeling she had nothing left, not even enough for herself.

"I guess we can look at it," Susan admitted, her pointed nose rising just a notch. The reluctance in her tone troubled Lisa. She sounded unwilling to give the cat up, unwilling to help them away from this trouble. What was she trying to stir up? Maybe she'd taken a sudden liking to the animal, even loved it. Lisa watched the prim, careful way Susan held the cat away from her skin, away from the soft orange hair falling down her back, and the stubborn clamp of her rouged lips. It was hard to believe Susan could love anything, suddenly or otherwise. But Jason—

No, that was too upsetting, thinking about them. Too upsetting for right now, when the last thing they needed was more upset. She sipped her cocoa; cooler now it tasted salty, thick, bordering on unpleasant, but she felt the need to finish it, to put at least that behind her. Lisa forced a dimple into her left cheek, rolled her eyes at Clare.

Humoring me, Clare thought. She pitied, envied, and despised that desperate good cheer. Staring straight ahead, she made an attempt at Lisa's expression. The effort was painful, like the splitting of a tight, dry scab. Her smile felt grotesque and stuck in place. She'd known this would happen. Things like this always happened. This is how they'd wanted it. They were stuck with it now because of them. She was stuck. Clare felt too hot and jerked at the neckline of her t-shirt, tried to make room to breathe. The group walked with slow, heavy steps, as if underwater.

"Here we are, here we are," Lisa exclaimed as they turned off the avenue onto Fourth Street. "It's right down there, behind that awning." Her voice sounded too high, and she tried to control it, force it back down to calm. Clare sometimes missed the meaning of what was said to her, but she could sense moods, especially hostility, panic, fear. The thing inside her sensed them, fed off them.

Lisa walked faster and fastest the rest of the way down the block. If only she could run away right now, leave Susan to her cat and Jason to Susan, Clare to that hidden part of herself. Leave all of them and run far, far away.

The lights were on but the door was barred, and the place didn't list any hours. There was a rough white stencil of a smiling cat on the glass window and a cluster of bells tied to the door, which would've rung if they could've opened it. Lisa and then Jason knocked and knocked and knocked on the glass door. The bells clanked against each other but didn't ring. There was no answer but the yowling of countless cats, the barking of a dog woken from sleep.

Clare muttered something too quickly for them to make out her exact wording, but Lisa understood and sympathized, tried to make the words natural for the others.

"She's right, guys. A lot of places might be closed for the night."

Susan sniffed loudly and Lisa knew she and Jason would hear about this later. One of Susan's many complaints was Lisa's translating for Clare, trying to make her strange comments fit in among healthy people. Susan believed in confrontation, in cruel to be kind, or sometimes just for the sake of cruel. She believed in hard truths and tough love. I can't understand what she's saying, she'd tell the others in front of Clare, as if Clare couldn't understand her. She doesn't make any sense.

Susan blamed Lisa for helping Clare along before her collapse, and after. She blamed Lisa for not confronting her, telling her she needed help again. But Lisa knew that cutting off communication with Clare would leave Clare to her greatest fear, a world where no one understood her, and she was unable to express anything. And the more this fear threatened her, the more Clare started to give way, to babble, to trail off in her words and let that other part of her become visible.

Lisa was only trying to help, to do what needed doing and no one else was willing or able to do. But which Clare was she helping, nurturing? What was that lurking thing doing while Lisa pretended everything was okay again? Biding its time, saving up its strength.

That was when being with Clare became unbearable. Lisa could hold out against the most hateful things Clare said to her, could talk her out of her most firmly held irrational beliefs, but she had to believe in what she was doing, had to know it was her friend and not the sickness she was fighting for. Lisa had to fight for herself, too, because she was the only one who could hold Clare up and all of them together, and she had no one to fall back on. If Lisa went under, they'd all come tumbling after.

"The phone number," Lisa murmured, with a relief she didn't dare trust. "There's a phone number on the door; we can call them." She disliked the smirk of certain victory on Susan's bony, precise face. How could Jason—kind, easygoing Jason with his broad jaw and broader grin, his gentle brown eyes—kiss a face like that? Susan didn't want them to leave the cat here, didn't want them to have it that easy. What did she want?

Jason got out his cell phone and dialed, let the connection ring over and over again. They could all hear the other end going off in the store, could hear it ringing and ringing and no one coming to answer it.

"Maybe they'll come back," Lisa offered. She had nothing else to give right now. "Maybe they'll come back soon. We could get a box or a basket or something and leave it in there, get it some milk... Even if it's in there overnight they'll come back in the morning and take it in. Don't you think...?" She didn't know where to look. Clare wasn't listening, or if she was, she wouldn't be able to help Lisa, wouldn't take her side now. Clare needed Lisa's support constantly, but was never in a position to give anything in return.

Lisa could tell Susan had shot down the idea before she'd had time to speak it, and Jason? She could barely look at him, let alone ask anything of him. He was lost and now wasn't the time to try and find him. The street was a long row of varying darknesses, interrupted in a few places by dimming lights as the last businesses closed, and planted with squat dark trees which seemed to grow upside down, sucking up the night sky through their blue-black branches.

"There'll be previews." The unexpected echo of Lisa's earlier reassurance caused them all to turn to Clare, then away again when she said nothing further. Susan sniffed and Jason looked embarrassed. Lisa began to feel alarmed. Why couldn't Clare stop obsessing about it? She needed to accept that it was past, that they weren't going to make it. They could go see the movie—she couldn't even remember which they'd meant to see—tomorrow night, or next week, or anytime, or not at all. But not tonight.

"Now what?" Jason asked, once he'd given up for good on calling.

"We can't just leave him here," Susan answered before Lisa had a chance to make the suggestion again. There was a kind of strain in her voice, too. She was invested in this rescue now, needed to see it through. Needed Jason to see her see it through, see that she wasn't the monster they thought she was. She had the feeling they'd all just as soon leave her out in a cardboard box along with the cat. It wasn't like she couldn't have found another apartment, even another boyfriend. She had the money and the charm and the looks. What threatened her was losing out in spite of those things. Waking up cold and missing something.

"Maybe the neighbors know when the rescue people will be back," Lisa suggested. She didn't really believe there was any chance of leaving the cat here tonight, but she needed them to believe in something, be working in some direction. She looked at the scrawny, limp grey cat, and couldn't summon up her usual love for animals. Try as she might, Lisa couldn't avoid the sense of something ominous, antagonistic to all of them, looking out those slit yellow eyes. If they talked to the neighbors they might be able to find out whose cat it was. At least there'd be someone else involved.

Susan was more than amenable to this suggestion. Why limit her audience to her roommates? Let everyone see her good intentions, her warm, selfless heart. And somewhere there was someone who would understand, take in this little creature, keep it, and the part of her that loved it, safe. "Where should we start?"

They started at the barbershop next door to the rescue center. The thin, anemic-looking young woman trimming the last customer's beard shrugged, but her stout, bulldog-faced client spoke up.

"If you're looking for a place to leave him 'til morning you'd best see the fellows in the repair shop across the street. They're the decentest folk on the block, they'll let him stay, sure."

Susan squealed out an effusive thanks and they left the barbershop, crossed the street.

Clare trailed after, uninvolved but still attached to the group. They were missing the movie, even right now at this moment they were missing it. She was missing everything and this was exactly how they'd wanted it, they'd known she'd be here, known she'd go to that café, they'd been waiting for it, had been and now they had her. She shouldn't have left her room tonight but it was too late now, too late for all of them. Should she try to warn Lisa?

Lisa noticed Clare watching her and tried to look the happy she couldn't feel right now. At least they were getting somewhere.

The sign on the door of the repair shop read 'Sorry—We're Closed,' but they could see three or four young men through the windows, hear warm laughter and conversation. Lisa had the inexplicable certainty that they were on her side.

Susan shrugged the cat onto one arm and knocked. A lanky, freckled young man answered it, gave the group a curious once-over.

"I'm sorry to be telling you this, but we're closed for the evening. It's tomorrow morning at ten you'll be wanting to come back if you've something you need fixed." He delivered the speech quickly, as if in a hurry to hear their reply.

Lisa looked the group over along with him; if they'd brought anything that needed fixing, they were hiding it pretty well. Anything these men could fix, anyway.

"Sorry to bother you. We don't need anything repaired," Lisa began, but Susan edged her out of the doorway and took over with a maudlin tale of cruel café owners, murderous cat-catchers and heartless rescuers. Bewildered or beguiled, the repairman shrugged and invited the party into the shop.

The other three men were seated on a workbench gesticulating at each other with bottles of Guinness, but they set these down and rose when the would-be rescuers came in, either because there were ladies present, or to get a better look.

"And are these friends of your'n, Mike?" one called to the man who'd admitted them.

"Does anyone know anyone who's lost a cat?" Lisa asked.

After much friendly and raucous debate, it was decided that the baker down the street had once kept a cat in his cellar to catch mice, but the cat had been an orange tabby, not a grey.

It was warm in the shop, but not stuffy. The light brogues and end-of-the-workday good cheer of the four repairmen reassured Lisa, gave her the sense that they were in good hands. The little stray would be too, if they could leave it with these men. She felt guilty for wanting to leave it with them—not just for wanting to be rid of it, no matter how—but for wanting to leave these kindly strangers with the small, tight sense of dread they'd picked up along with the stray. Still, she felt sure they'd be immune to it, were too strong and happy for that kind of trouble. It was only she and her friends who were weak, susceptible to this new threat. She turned to Clare, couldn't get her smile returned in kind.

Clare watched the untied lace of one sneaker, not looking up as friendly introductions went around, but letting Lisa give her name for her. Yes, Lisa would take care of everything, she could trust Lisa. For now. Clare had the sense of something very important being discussed, but she couldn't make out quite what. Something about staying, or was it going? It didn't matter. Too late, already too late. She was already here and it was too late. If only this could be the end of it, but they'd got her good now.

"I'll wait outside." Better there than here. A better chance of getting away.

"Sure, go ahead." Lisa was glad Clare couldn't tell how happy she was to have her out of sight, not to have to worry about every small change in her expression, every stray spark that might trigger an explosion.

Their imposition on these men embarrassed her. Here they were, resting after a long day's work, and Susan was bothering them about some stranger's lost cat, when all they wanted was to go home and get a decent night's sleep. By all rights, it wasn't even their stray to look after. They hadn't been the first ones to see it; it had been in the café before they arrived. Lisa felt as if they'd stolen a trouble they had no real claim to, and were now trying to pass it off as genuine. She tried to give a succinct explanation and ask if the stray could stay in the store until morning, but she couldn't compete with the spectacle of Susan.

Crooning to her beneficiary, making eyes at everything from the front door to the rack of bicycles in the back, and inventing an epic with herself as heroine, Susan was truly in her element. She invited the men to pet the kitten, bending low to move it from lap to lap, giggling and pouting by turns. At least some people appreciated her. She'd been spending too much time around the kind of people who'd leave something weak and soft and helpless for dead, too much time with someone who didn't know what he wanted, no matter how hard Susan tried to be whatever that was.

Jason tossed Lisa an are-you-getting-this look, and was surprised to receive in return a radiant smile, the longest green-light gaze she'd given him since he started dating Susan. Just for a moment, it seemed ridiculous, a bad joke, that he should be with that simpering flirt instead of Lisa. Who was Susan trying to impress, really.

Lisa had no time to reproach herself for looking too long at Jason, in her joy at finally being able to again. That had always been her favorite sign of their closeness, the real proof of it for her—the way each could sense what the other was thinking, the way they could discuss anything with a glance. After they rode with Clare to the hospital, Lisa had been afraid to look at Jason, afraid to see her own fear in his.

But maybe it had been Jason who was too afraid. He and Lisa had visited together at first, but then his work schedule began to interfere—or he said it did—and Lisa had to go alone. Clare had told her everything, everything that wasn't really, but *was* when she spoke it into Lisa's thoughts with that dull, unbreaking stare. Lisa had been afraid of Clare, afraid of having to be with her, and afraid of her own weakness for wanting to run away from that. To run away from her friend.

Walking back down First Avenue, Lisa had gotten soaked by a chill, heavy rain, but she'd felt numb before she left the hospital. Construction crews cordoned off her path home and the East River was a wide-open mouth too close to her, ready to swallow. Everything was made of grey sky and wet cement, and Lisa's steps seemed not to move her forward, only to wear her out. She'd used up all the warmth she was capable of on Clare, didn't have enough to keep herself going. When she got back, Jason wrapped a blanket around her shoulders and sat next to her on the couch, rubbed her arms and shoulders until she felt something like alive again. You're pale as death, he told her. Do you want to talk about it? And she'd said, I don't know if I can.

Watching Jason watching Susan, Lisa twisted nervous, dark strands of hair, tucked them away among the tangles behind her ears. She had the sense of needing to act now or risk losing where they were and everything that could come after.

I wish I could be there for her, Jason had told her. I hate myself for not being there for her more. But I am here for you, Lisa. You're not alone in this, okay? Don't you forget that. And then they'd talked about the future, about what they'd do when everything was good again, until they almost believed in it.

Lisa had felt as if the two of them had been away a long time, ever since Clare lost Mark, maybe, but they were now on the point of coming home again, already in the driveway and a few steps from the door. And because of what she and Jason had with each other, when she looked up at him she'd known she didn't have to tell him. They were both crying a little, just from emotional overexertion, and trying to hide it. Jason was doing an even worse job than Lisa, but grinning and bearing it, keeping a firm arm around her shoulders.

I'm so lucky to have you, Lisa began. She'd wanted to end with 'in my life,' but only made it as far as 'in the apartment'. But then she'd thrown caution to a passing draft and told him, there's no one I'd rather be with than you.

Later she'd hated herself for saying it that way. What did it mean? No one she'd rather live with, no one she'd rather be with at this moment, or no one she'd rather be with, in every way and always, really *be* with? She couldn't know which she'd meant any more than she could know which Jason had heard. But he'd told her, right back at you, Lisa. Right back at you.

Jason watched his girlfriend dandling the limp grey cat from knee to knee, talking about what an animal lover she was, and wondered what she hoped to get out of it. She wasn't making him jealous, if that was her deal, or making herself more attractive to him. If she wanted a different guy, fine, but why pursue one—not one, four—in front of him? This was obviously a performance of some kind. And in its way, an effective one. When he turned back to Lisa, she, too, was watching Susan, much the way an understudy watches the primadonna, though with less malice. The setting struck him as inconvenient. For once he had a clear view of it all, was ready to evict Susan in every sense, and here they were in a closed repair shop on Saturday night, negotiating room and board for a stray cat. He watched Lisa until he knew she could feel it— she didn't look back, but her eyes crept to the dusty floor, and she colored with the effort of pretending not to notice.

Well how about that. Maybe she really was up for something. And why not? Lisa, the good, better, best friend, the girl with the coolest taste in alternative music and black-and-white cinema, not too long ago the closest he'd ever felt to anybody. And Susan? When you got down to it, the girl was a footnote, something you could read the whole text without stopping to notice. She wasn't important and wouldn't be memorable. They'd been sleeping together three months and never said 'I love you,' never wanted to. At least he hadn't, and he wasn't betting on Susan holding back any deeper feelings. Could he do it right now, or as soon as they left the store? Why the hell not. He'd do it nicely—no use making a scene in front of Lisa and Clare—he'd just tell her he was sorry, but this was the last straw... What, the cat?

"Thank you sooooo much," Susan was purring to lanky, freckled Mike, who'd agreed to take the cat home with him and bring it to the rescue in the morning. Lisa was surprised and relieved. If Clare wanted, they could even make the later showing of the movie. But the warm interior of the shop made Lisa drowsy, and she was paying more attention to Jason than to Susan. She looked at him again now, found him still looking at her, looking with a kind of dare in his eyes, an invitation.

Someone knocked at the front door and the cat squirmed and scratched Susan. She cursed and almost dropped it, caught it by its tail. It yowled and clutched at her dress while she tried to pin its legs down and keep a smile on her face.

"Guess I'd better be answering that." Mike went to the door. Lisa glanced at Jason, gave him a what-next raise of her eyebrows. He closed the two-step distance between them and put a hand on her shoulder, as if to strengthen her against some imminent danger. No one in the shop doubted that the visitor had something to do with the cat. Anything else was just too unlikely. They strained to hear the discussion in the doorway.

Jason's touch on her shoulder was a hell of indecision for Lisa. How easy it would be to grab his hand, grab all of him, and refuse to let go. She'd felt it, for the first time since last winter she'd felt them close again, and she knew she couldn't feel it alone—it was a two-person emotion. What did she have to lose if she told him right now that—but how could she? Getting rid of the stray didn't change anything. Susan was still there.

Lisa had already guessed the next guest by the time he identified himself. The stout, swarthy baker with his dusty apron and implacable scowl gave the night a farcical feel: He was too much a picture-book villain to actually be involved.

"Who have my cat?" he bellowed in the indignant tone of a matron whose purse has been snatched in broad daylight. No one answered him; the matter seemed self-explanatory. Lisa didn't like the sneer on Susan's face, but she wasn't worried. It wasn't their problem anymore. Either this was the cat's rightful owner, or it wasn't. That was a matter for Mike and his friends and the shelter and the baker and whoever else to solve, not them. They had their own worries. If Susan wanted to borrow trouble she could go right outside. Clare certainly had plenty, plenty of worry and fear and darkness to give away.

That had been what Lisa feared that night with Jason: She'd been afraid of becoming like Clare, a source of contagion and negativity, toxic to herself and everyone she touched. Jason had said he wanted to help her, wanted to be there for her, but she wasn't willing to ask so much of him. Better to sacrifice her own happiness for his, for Clare's. Better to hurt him in the short run, and protect him from what she had to go through for the rest of them. But she'd only meant to put them off a little while, until Clare was better and they were all happy. What a long time that turned out to be.

Jason had wrapped his arms around Lisa that night, pressed a kiss into the top of her hairline. Had held her a few moments, just so, making himself a wall around her. How good, how right that had felt. How safe. Like coming in from a storm, exhausted, and falling into your own warm bed. He could protect her from anything, from all of it, she was sure.

And then just like that, she wasn't. She thought of the secret, horrible, guilty dread she felt every time she went to see Clare, and the idea of Jason ever feeling that way towards her was unbearable. She thought of how Mark must have felt, nursing Clare through this the last time, knowing she might never really be well again. How it must have driven him from her. No, she decided. She couldn't be with Jason until she was in a position to make him happy.

Jason had let her lean back against him, bent to put just the softest pressure on her lips, and her first response had been, I can't right now. There hadn't been much more to say and they'd left it like that, gone on like nothing had happened, and then the next thing that happened was they couldn't make the rent, and Lisa's classmate Susan was looking for a sublet, was new and sexy and completely separate from the way things had been.

"This cat is clearly grey," Susan repeated over the heated grumbling of the baker.

"I know he grey! He my cat!" He looked ready to tear it from her, if there weren't a half dozen sheepish onlookers in the room.

"As I understand it," Susan spoke crisply, as if to emphasize the baker's inarticulateness, "you're missing an *orange* cat."

"I have orange cat. Then I have grey cat. This cat."

"Susan," Lisa began, but she knew it was useless. It was all useless. Even if they got the cat to the shelter, this man could just pick it up in the morning. What difference did it make whether they gave it to him now or then?

"What happened to the orange cat," Susan more accused than asked the baker.

"He run away. Then I get this cat."

Susan gave a gloating look around the room. Two cats run away? Clearly this man was unfit to take care of an animal. Thank goodness she was here. Not Lisa, not Jason, certainly not Clare— She, Susan, had rescued the little creature, and she'd be damned if she was going to be cheated of that.

Taking in Susan's expression, Lisa sighed. They were going to be here a while. She should go check on Clare. It didn't seem safe to leave Clare alone at night with— herself. But Lisa felt so, so tired, thinking of all they'd have to go through to take care of this small, mewing curse, and it seemed to her that Jason's hand on her shoulder was the only thing keeping her standing. In a few minutes, she'd have to break away from him, go check on Clare. Just a few more minutes.

"Jason?" But before he could answer her murmured appeal, the front door swung open, no knock this time.

"Oh, good, you've still got him." The bulldog-faced man was now neatly shaven. The baker threw up his short hairy arms at the interruption, and Lisa empathized. With a doleful shake of his jowls, the new entry introduced two short-haired women in leather jackets and their mid-thirties, who lived next door to the bakery. Two of Mike's coworkers rose again to offer them seats, which they didn't accept.

"Yeah, I figure that's Tony's cat," the stouter of the two women offered. Her teeth had heavy nicotine stains and there was something aggressive in her tone.

Lisa could see they hadn't come to make peace. "Jason?" she asked again. He tightened his grip on her shoulder, but didn't answer.

"I heard that thing yowling all day and night down in that cellar. He don't take any care of it, right, Missy?"

The thinner of the two, with an artificial cherry tint to her hair, nodded in agreement, then shook her head at the baker, who threw up his hands again.

"Listen, girly, don't give that man the cat," the stouter woman advised Susan, who in no way needed to hear it. "He don't take care of it at all."

"It *my* cat!" the baker insisted, though that no longer seemed to be the matter in question.

Lisa wondered who'd come in next. How could this still be their problem, with half the block here to weigh in on it? That look on Clare's face, when Susan had first picked up the cat—almost as if she'd known something. Clare. How long had it been? "Jason, I think we should go," she told him, under the rising whirl of voices in the now too-warm shop.

"We can't just leave Susan here," he replied, begging her to tell him they could.

"Susan can come with us." But she didn't look him in the face as she spoke these last words, because she didn't believe them herself.

"You know she won't."

They were silent again. Again Susan had won, had been the one Jason wanted to be with and stay with. Lisa wondered how that happened, how it had happened the first time, and every day since, that Jason wanted Susan and not her. Not that Susan wasn't beautiful and charming and superior to her in so many ways. Not that she didn't see how lots of guys could fall for Susan. It was just Jason doing it that surprised her. She knew she couldn't compete with Susan in any conventional way, but she and Jason had been so close, had understood each other so well—she thought that had meant more to him. But it hadn't, and maybe she hadn't understood him as well as she'd thought.

What was it about Susan? Jason had been around plenty of pretty—even prettier—girls before Susan, and never gotten involved. Lisa had let herself think he was waiting—but of course he hadn't been. Then, a couple weeks after the only indication he'd ever given her of wanting to be more than friends, Susan had moved into Clare's room, and it was hard for Lisa and Jason to find time alone together. Susan always seemed to be hovering around Jason's space in the living room, and Lisa thought it would be rude for them to go into her bedroom and shut Susan out, rude not to welcome this newcomer.

Maybe Susan feels lonely, she'd thought. Maybe she feels left out that she isn't as close with us as we are with each other. But then she noticed that Susan never tagged along, never popped in, when it was just Lisa alone, that Susan was only interested in getting closer to Jason. In her private conversations with Lisa, he always came up, and Lisa could tell Susan was trying to gauge their relationship, to see what she was allowed. Then one day she'd asked, point blank, whether Lisa would mind if she went for Jason.

Lisa had okayed it. Had said she didn't mind, because she didn't think she had a right to. Besides, she'd known—at the time—that Jason would never go for Susan. Susan was the kind of girl he and Lisa would've laughed at in private: superficial, thoughtless, totally without interests, opinions, or ambitions. When Susan first moved in, Lisa had had to stand up for her behind her back, when Jason made too much fun of her. Later, she wished she could ask him when he stopped minding those things about Susan.

It had only taken until January for Jason and Susan to get involved. Casual, at first—just flirtation, the occasional teasing kiss. Lisa had been sure it wouldn't last. Just until Clare gets back, she'd told herself, as if that would solve everything. She'd been certain that when Clare got back and Susan had to move out of her room, Susan would go away altogether, leave their apartment and not be a problem anymore. And Lisa and Jason would look back and laugh.

But Clare had been gone a long, long time, well into the new year, and they'd stopped talking about Susan finding somewhere else to live. Lisa had worried for Clare, worried that she'd come out of the hospital and not have anywhere to go. When she visited in the ward, Lisa put out extra cheer about the apartment, how lovely Susan was, how much fun they'd have together when Clare came back. Lisa always said, when you come back, not, when they let you out. As if it were Clare's decision when to come, and they were all just waiting for her to make up her mind and do it.

Then Clare had finally gotten out and there had come the new living arrangements, getting rid of half the furniture in the living room, installing a big new bed and a curtain for the privacy Jason had never needed on his own. Susan had moved her things from Clare's bedroom to Jason's, and still Lisa kept waiting for the time when things would be like before.

Lisa thought of the cat coming into their home as Susan had, innocuous at first— just temporary—then taking over. What else would change? For all the heated arguing going on in the already overheated shop, for all the accusations the neighbors were throwing at the baker, they didn't seem to have any suggestions as to what to do with the cat, and weren't offering to take it themselves. Mike had been willing to sit the cat overnight, but wasn't going to face off such controversy.

"I bet old lady Perkins would take it," the stout, nicotine-tinted woman in the leather jacket broke in. "She's already got three cats. Somebody run and see if Mrs. Perkins from 3B's still up."

One of the repairman obeyed. The baker followed, threatening alternately to summon his wife and the police. Lisa stood, unable to get a grip on Jason or anything in the eye of this storm, and watched Susan. She watched the forgettable grey sack of bones and claws slung squirming over Susan's thin arm, and was surprised by a feeling the closest she'd ever had to hatred. There was no way out, and she was tired, so tired she could hardly stand, hardly even keep breathing in all this heat and noise. The whole thing was so ridiculous she wanted to skip laughter and go straight to tears.

"I'm going to check on Clare," she told Jason, not sure if he heard. When she pulled out from under his grip, he called, "Wait," but she couldn't, no matter how much she wanted to. Someone had to take care of Clare, and she'd already waited too long. Soon, very soon, in just a few minutes, she'd come back for Jason. Soon it would all be like it had before the cat, and maybe not long after that, it would be like it had before Susan.

Outside the store it was cool, cool and dry the way the rest of the house feels when you come out of a steamy shower. Lisa stepped out of the way to let pass the baker, a stringy middle-aged woman with a matching apron and a runny nose, the repairman, and a grey-haired matron supported by a wooden cane and a small boy in Superman pajamas. When the door closed behind the newcomers, it was quiet, their senseless arguing a removed whir to match the traffic on the avenues. What did they want, all those people in there? What were they trying to do? They must believe in something, to keep fighting the way they did.

Lisa looked up and down the dark, empty block, whose last light was the door she'd just stepped out of, and realized she'd known Clare would be gone. She'd waited too long to go after her, or maybe any amount of time would've been too long. It had come out and carried Clare away, and Lisa had let it.

Lisa got out her cell phone and dialed Clare, let it ring. She knew it was useless. Clare had left and Lisa didn't know how to follow her. She was so tired, only wanted to go home, with or without the others. But she had to look for Clare, because no one else would. And because she had let that thing take Clare away, had wanted to be rid of her and let her go, knowing. Lisa had known from that look of Clare's that something like this was coming, and she had let it happen.

A part of her that she couldn't—wasn't allowed to, wouldn't—listen to, asked, wasn't this what you wanted? Clare gone, and the thing you were afraid of with her? Lisa hadn't wanted Clare out of her life, but she'd learned that the two were impossible to separate, Clare and the sickness. Lisa started walking, taking every step in spite of her weakness, in spite of the shameful part of her that had wished Clare away all those fearful, confusing months since she'd first left. Lisa would find her, even if that meant finding the disease instead of her friend, because they were one and the same. She'd find her even though it meant leaving Jason now, giving up on him again and maybe for good this time.

She gave a last look at the crowd tucked into the shop among the old bicycles and spare parts. The glass was beginning to fog up, to hide that busy world from Lisa. They'd keep fighting forever, because they were determined to save what couldn't be. Just a few steps to lose sight of them. Where would Clare go? Lisa asked herself, ignoring one, two, three phone calls from Jason. I just have to think like Clare.

They didn't make the late showing, either.

***

It was a lazy Sunday afternoon and the cat had kept Jason up again, but he was starting to get used to it. Besides, it was sweet how Susan adored the little devil. He looked at her now, graceful in her pink silk nightie, stroking the thin grey animal, which now wore a black collar with a bell and their address. The curving rose design peeked out over the pink lace on Susan's chest. It had healed nicely, no dead skin left. The cat purred and the sun seeped softly through their curtain and everything on this side of it was alright, it was right that Susan was here.

Susan watched Jason out of the edges of her narrowed eyes, keeping her gaze on the cat. She knew she had him this time, that they were safe now. All the rest had been nonsense, some kind of confusion about ideals and trying to play the good guy. The cat purred her contentment for her: She was the one who would stay when the others were gone, the one who wasn't temporary or replaceable or an outsider, the one who belonged. And Jason was completely hers, as much as if she'd collared and belled him, too.

"I love you, Jason," she purred, not raising her eyes from the cat, not needing to.

"Right back at you, Susan," Jason told her, running a hand through his well-groomed brown hair. "Right back at you."

The front door opened and closed, and then the door to Lisa's bedroom. Visiting hours must be over. Jason never asked how Clare was doing anymore. He'd stopped asking about Lisa, too. She seemed distant lately; after the end of this lease they wouldn't live together again. It'd been a while since he considered them close friends. He'd been sad about that, regretted losing Lisa, but sometimes people just grow apart. He and Susan had each other, and that was enough.

In her bedroom, Lisa lay face down on her comforter, tried to steady her breathing, to exhale all the horrible things she'd heard that morning. Tomorrow at the same time, she'd go back, because she was the only one Clare had, the only thing other than the sickness that would always be with her. Clare had gotten fragile again and Lisa feared she wouldn't be enough to feed the thing inside of her much longer. Which one of them would it take next? But she already knew the answer to that.

Knew it and wanted more than anything to stay away, but couldn't, couldn't leave her friend alone. She allowed herself a count of fifteen, and then got up again, patted her close-cropped hair back into place. She had things to do, couldn't afford to waste the time. The pink clock on the counter had said she was running a half hour late, but she should've expected that. It had already been too late the first time Clare went away.

A fine row of hairs stood up along the cat's back, but Susan stroked it back to sleep.

About the Author

Kat Hausler is the youngest of four siblings, and grew up in Northern Virginia. She spent several years in and around Greenwich Village while studying German and Creative Writing at New York University, but since 2008 resides in Berlin, where she writes, teaches English, and is studying to become a certified translator.

ALL THINGS THAT MATTER PRESS ™

FOR MORE INFORMATION ON TITLES AVAILABLE FROM
ALL THINGS THAT MATTER PRESS, GO TO
http://allthingsthatmatterpress.com
or contact us at
allthingsthatmatterpress@gmail.com

3498374

Made in the USA